Drachengott 1

Wind

KJ Taylor

Shooting Star Press

First Edition 2022

Shooting Star Press,
PO Box 6813,
Charnwood ACT 2615

info@shootingstar.pub
www.shootingstar.pub

ABN 63 158 506 524

ISBN 978-1-925821-56-7 (pbk)

ISBN 978-1-925821-57-4(ebook)

A catalogue record for this book is available from the National Library of Australia.

Cover and Art by Sarah Beurfeind at Six Rabbits Illustration

Cover design by SSP

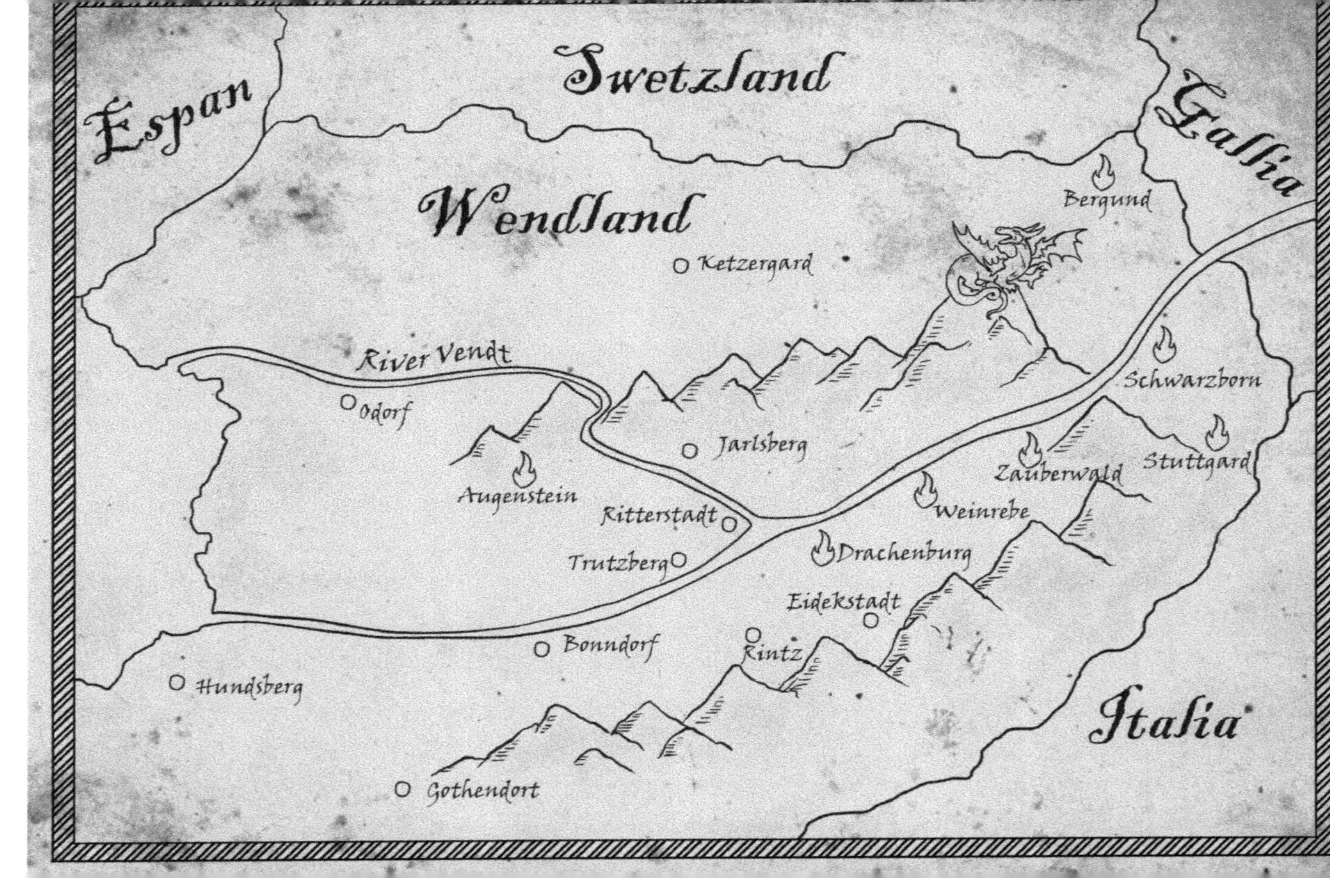

Espan
Swetzland
Gallia
Wendland
Bergund
Ketzergard
River Vendt
Schwarzborn
Odorf
Jarlsberg
Augenstein
Zauberwald
Stuttgard
Ritterstadt
Weinrebe
Trutzberg
Drachenburg
Eidekstadt
Bonndorf
Rintz
Hundsberg
Italia
Gothendort

Chapter 1

The wind whistled through the darkness, shaking the branches all about and putting a chill into the air. It carried a scent with it, straight to Rutger's nose. He took it in and immediately tensed.

'Did you smell that, Horst?' he hissed, snatching his older brother by the arm.

Horst shook him off. 'Not now, Rut — we're in enough trouble without worrying about funny smells.'

'But it smells like rotting meat!' Rutger insisted. He paused, ignoring Horst's impatient look, and breathed in deeply. The smell hit him again — worse, this time. He retched slightly. 'Can't you smell it?'

Horst, big and muscular, turned his head in the gloom and sniffed. A moment later, he grimaced. 'You're right: something's dead out there. Come on, let's move on before we find out what.'

He strode off, Rutger hurrying after him. 'You don't think it's spiders, do you?'

'Could be,' Horst said shortly. 'Keep your eyes open.'

Rutger swallowed and put a hand on the hilt of the long dagger looped through his belt. He had never seen a giant spider before, and he wanted to keep it that way. Silently, he wished he had never asked to come out here into the forest with Horst. But it had all seemed so harmless — just a quick stroll through the forest to check Horst's mink traps. But then they hadn't been able to find the last trap, and now they were lost.

I really am the unlucky seventh son, he thought glumly.

If Horst was as worried as his brother, he didn't show it. He walked slightly ahead, dead mink swinging from his belt. A big old woodaxe hung on his back, brought along for protection. Night was falling now, and the sooner they got out of here the better.

The forest all around was dense and looked threatening, its spiky pine needles sighing in the relentless wind. Night always seemed to come early here. But at least the putrid smell had gone away.

'How close do you think we are now?' Rutger asked in a low voice.

Horst shook his head. 'Not sure — I think there's a clearing up ahead, though.'

Rutger came to his brother's side, and the two of them climbed a small rise into the clearing. The instant Rutger left the shelter of the trees, it hit him again: the hideous stench of rotting meat slamming into his nose, so powerfully that his eyes watered. Beside him, Horst had stopped. Rutger heard him swear softly. He looked up, intending to tell his brother that they should go — and then he saw it.

Ahead, in the clearing, a faint light began to glow. It shone on the dark, lumpy shapes which hung from the trees at the far side. Some could have been animal corpses, but the rest ...

Horst wrenched the axe down off his back. 'Get behind me, Rut,' he said sharply. 'Get out of here. Now.'

'What—?' Rutger started to say — but too late.

As the light brightened, two of the hanging shapes dropped to the ground and stepped forward. They wore rough leather tunics with hoods which covered their heads, but on each of their chests was a pair of red gemstones, each , set into an amulet. They glowed faintly in the light, making a halo over each of the two men, like a pair of glowering eyes.

'Jüngen!' Rutger heard himself say.

One of the pair pointed accusingly at them. 'How dare you enter this sacred grove?'

Horst started to back away, axe raised.

The two Jüngen joined hands, and the light around them intensified as their linked hands rose. An instant later, a great flash blinded Rutger. He cried out as he fell back, but his voice was drowned out by a screeching roar from above.

A pitch-black dragon was hovering over the Jüngen's heads, its eyes glowing red. Light crackled over its wings, and it roared again.

The Jüngen let go of each other, and the second of the two spoke to the dragon. His words were a short, cold command.

'Kill them.'

The dragon snarled, and launched itself across the clearing. One moment it was hovering, the next it was rushing straight at Rutger and Horst, fangs and talons gleaming.

Horst lurched sideways and swung his axe at the creature, catching it in the side of the head. The dragon veered away and made a clumsy landing, but then shook itself and charged.

'Run!' Horst yelled at Rutger.

Rutger managed to free his dagger. 'No!'

Horst swore again and lashed out with his axe, holding the dragon at bay. It kept back, avoiding the blade.

'Kill!' one of its summoners insisted.

The dragon growled, and made a sudden lunge. Its jaws snapped shut around Horst's waist. He bellowed and started to hack at the beast's head. Rutger stood frozen for an instant, but when he saw blood start to stain his brother's tunic his fear left him. Shouting, he raised his dagger and rushed in.

The dragon's wing hit him in the side of the head, making him step back before slashing at it again. This time, his dagger cut through the pale membrane of the wing, and silvery blood splattered over his arm. Rutger gasped at the heat of it, but, before he could attack again, another roar split the air as the dragon let go of Horst. It backed away, shaking its head, and Rutger saw that one of its long, curving horns had snapped clean in half. Freed, Horst stumbled to his knees, one hand still clutching his axe and the other reaching down to touch his wound. The broken horn lay on the ground not far away.

Rutger ran up to his brother. 'Horst, are you all right?'

Horst groaned as Rutger helped him up. 'We can't win this — we have to escape.'

Rutger bent and snatched up the horn. Nearby, the dragon had already recovered itself. Its burning eyes fell on the horn in Rutger's hand, and it snarled.

'Come on,' Rutger told Horst, 'lean on me.'

He pulled Horst's free arm over his shoulders, and started to help him away. Grimacing, Horst managed to stand upright. But the dragon was too fast for them. It made another charge across the clearing toward them — and then stopped in its tracks. It hesitated, head turning to stare into the gloom. Something rustled in the darkness.

The dragon's eyes narrowed, and it started to growl. Rutger and Horst stopped to look at the beast for an instant, then turned to make their escape, just as something massive came bursting into the clearing.

Rutger caught a brief glimpse of huge, hairy legs, their tips clawed, reaching out in a quick scooping motion. They caught hold of him and Horst, dragging them backward. Hurled to the ground, claws needling through the skin on his back, Rutger saw the dragon struggling as a second monster seized it and began to take the beast for its own. Rutger struggled, too, but, trapped against Horst's collapsed body, it was hopeless, and the gigantic spider pulled them both into cloying darkness.

Rutger couldn't see anything, but he felt the moment when the spider bit. The sudden impact of the fangs juddered through Horst and into his own body. Horst grunted with pain, and somewhere the dragon screeched.

And then there was light again — blazing, silvery light — and heat. The spider's grip slackened.

Rolling over, Rutger saw flames licking the trees above and around him. Behind him the spider was retreating, clicking its distress. Hair shrivelling in the heat, it retreated. Nearby the other spider had fallen back as well, leaving the dragon on the ground. The two Jüngen were already backing away.

Rutger stooped to help Horst, eyes on the dragon. But the creature didn't come at them again. Two bloody puncture wounds oozed on its back, and its breathing sounded hoarse and edged with pain. The fire it had breathed was already starting to die down, and the spider that had attacked it had begun a cautious return. More spiders were emerging from the darkness, out of reach of the flames.

The dragon looked toward its summoners, and a voice came out of the air; pained, weak and — Rutger started — female.

Help me!

The two Jüngen hesitated, both watching the returning spiders. One made a move toward the dragon, but the other grabbed his arm. 'Forget it: it's done for. Let's get out of here.'

The dragon watched them flee. *Curse you!* she screamed.

Rutger shook Horst by the shoulder. 'Horst, get up — we have to run!'

Horst stirred. 'Run, Rut,' he whispered. 'Save yourself.'

Rutger turned him over, and saw the fang marks on Horst's upper chest. 'No,' he said stupidly. 'You can't—'

Horst's breath had already become laboured, wheezing in his lungs. Sweat beaded on his face. 'Go,' he whispered again. 'I'm done for ... Get out of here ... now.'

Rutger started to sob. 'I can't leave you.'

'You have to,' said Horst. He took in a slow, rattling breath. 'Look after ... the others ... Tell them what happened. For me. Please.'

All around the edges of the clearing, the spiders were closing in. The dragon lay gasping on her back, not far from where the stinking corpses hung. The two Jüngen had already vanished.

Rutger knew he had no choice. 'I'll tell them,' he promised. He had lost his dagger, but Horst's axe lay nearby. Scooping it up, he ran, swinging the weapon wildly to fend off the spiders, who, sensing living prey, had turned to chase him – and left Horst and the dragon to their fates.

*

Horst heard Rutger's retreating footsteps. His body had gone numb, but he managed to roll over and watch his brother's dark shape vanish into the night. With his last strength, Horst muttered a prayer for his brother's safety. Nearby, he could hear the dragon's rasping breaths mingling with his own, and he knew that the spider's venom must have weakened the creature as badly as it had him. Not that it mattered — any moment now, the spiders would close in and drag them both away. If he was lucky, he would be dead by the time they came to suck out his innards.

But the fatal blow did not come. He looked up through wavering vision, and saw a spider looming over him — but then it was retreating again, driven away by a lance of white fire. The dragon had pulled herself upright, snarling as she spat her flames. This time, they hit the nearest spider directly. It caught alight, and started to writhe, thrashing in agony as its shell withered and cracked in the heat. Encouraged, the dragon lifted her head and sent a fireball at a second spider. It, too, caught alight, and ran away back into the forest, setting several trees on fire along the way. It was enough to finally send the rest of the spiders away to seek less dangerous prey.

Once they had gone, an eerie silence fell in the clearing. The dragon, energy spent, let her head droop to the ground.

Horst dragged himself toward her, thinking that he might live a little longer if she was nearby. But he didn't have the strength to get far. About an arm's length from the creature, he collapsed and lay on his side. The clearing spun around him, lurching hideously whenever he tried to move. His limbs had started to stiffen now as the paralysis spread, and everything had begun to go dark. Weak and confused, he slipped away into what he thought was death.

But the world came back a few moments later; he opened his eyes and stared ahead, disorientated.

After a little while, he realised that a pair of red eyes were staring back. The dragon was beside him, flanks slowly heaving, neck lying flat along the ground. But her eyes were open, and fixed on him; a dim light in the gloom.

Horst returned her stare, thinking nothing in particular. He couldn't seem to move.

Then the dragon's voice came again, speaking out of the air. It sounded weak.

What ... are you?

Horst's tongue felt swollen. 'I'm a man,' he mumbled.

The dragon looked at him, then stared away toward the woods. *So were they.*

'Jüngen,' said Horst.

She turned her head to look at him again. *What do they worship?*

Horst struggled to answer. 'The ... Drachengott,' he managed. 'Him. He gives them powers.'

The dragon's eyes burned. *They left me to die*, her voice hissed.

Horst said nothing, puzzled. 'Don't you know ... what you are?' he asked at last.

The dragon stared at him.

Horst looked away, in the direction Rutger had gone. 'Didn't want it to be like this,' he whispered. His throat felt as though it were closing. 'My wife ... my daughters ... Who's going to...?'

But he couldn't speak any more after that. The last of his voice faded, and his vision faded as well. A coldness spread through his body, and his will to hold on slipped away. The last thing he saw was the dragon's eyes, glowing in the darkness, and then he was gone.

Chapter 2

A mixture of pain and fear gripped the dragon as she lay there, paralysed by venom. She watched Horst, her only companion in this place, and sensed the moment when his life left him. She felt no malice toward him, only vague curiosity, and even a touch of sadness. She wondered who he had been and where he had gone. But wherever it was, she could feel herself being pulled there now, and she had no more strength to resist. She closed her eyes, and quietly surrendered.

Yet she did not fall into the darkness she had expected, but into a dream. One moment she was lying on the forest floor, unable to move, and the next she was flying. The wind slid over her wings and she soared, legs tucked in under her belly, spiked tail rigid behind her.

She was not alone. Around her other dragons began to appear, dropping from the stormy clouds above to fly at her side. Some were green, some white, some brown or grey, or sky blue. But none of them had her burning blood-red eyes.

Below, a range of mountains sheltered a long valley where houses clustered. At the far end of the valley, looming above it all, was a mountain bigger than any other: colossal, craggy, its dark rock sides showing not a trace of snow in spite of its height.

Unable to control what direction she took, the dragon did not fly to the mountain's peak as she wanted to, but instead followed the others downward as they flew to the mountain's base. Landing on a chunk of granite amongst the lush vegetation, she perched there while the others landed around her.

Around her were people, at least a hundred of them, all wearing red gemstones. They were laying baskets of food at the mountain's base, bowing low and murmuring prayers, while the dragons watched in silence. But the black dragon's eyes were drawn to one human in particular — a woman who was standing apart. As her fellows turned to go, she glanced up at the mountain, and the dragon saw the hard, hateful look on her pale face.

She followed the woman's gaze, and, as the dream began to fade, she saw it: saw the entire mountaintop shift, saw ridges crack and break away under talons the size of ancient tree trunks — and the head of a dragon big enough to swallow the world slowly rose into the sky.

*

Cold greeted the black dragon when she woke up. As she opened her eyes, she groaned. Her body was stiff, and everything ached from her talons to the tip of her tail. But she was alive. Her limbs throbbed, but they would obey her. She breathed in and hissed the breath back out again. She was not going to die after all — she was going to live. And as the dream stirred in her memory, she knew what she had to do.

Slowly and clumsily, she got up,. Some traces of venom must have lingered in her system – the world began to spin slowly around her. She shook her head angrily, and the dizziness began to wear off. She spread her wings and flapped them a couple of times to loosen them up. Morning had come, and she could see blue sky above the clearing. If she was careful, she might be able to make it up there. She reared onto her hind legs and flapped her wings again, harder this time. Her injured membrane oozed a little blood, but the wing could still catch the air, and she began to rise from the ground. Encouraged, she flapped more vigorously, rising almost straight upward out of the clearing. The trees fell away below her, and then she was in the air.

There, she flew in a slow circle while she got her bearings. The forest spread out below in every direction, covering a large range of hills. But to the south it gave way to fields at the foot of the hills, pale green against the brown-black of the treeline. From here she could see buildings, a little like those in her dream, and she flew toward them. However, quickly she realised that they were not the human houses she had dreamed of. Once she was over them, she flew lower, circling slowly so she could take it all in.

A sprawl of small homes and larger buildings, all protected by a wall of sharpened logs. People were everywhere, and she heard them shouting as they ran about, alarmed by the sight of her. Already some of them were seizing weapons. The dragon flew higher to avoid them; she had no interest in fighting them. But as she retreated, she caught a brief glimpse of one human in particular — a human standing in a doorway, one hand clutching an axe. In the other he held something sharp and silvery.

Rutger, the dragon breathed. *I see you.*

Then she turned and flew away, to begin her search for the mountain of the Drachengott.

*

It took the black dragon five days to find the mountain. But somehow, even though she had no memory of anything before the moment of her summoning, she knew exactly which way to go. Leaving Rutger's village behind, she flew up over the forested hills, and followed the line of the hills eastward. Her journey had begun.

The hills went on for a long way, eventually shedding the forest and giving way to grazelands; great expanses of green grass where flocks of sheep and goats browsed. They scattered in fight when the dragon's shadow fell over them, but she left them alone. Even though she had not eaten, she felt no hunger pains.

In the lowlands on either side of the hills, she saw human settlements, surrounded by farmland. Every town and village was surrounded by walls. And the further east she went, the grimmer things seemed to become. The settlements grew thinner on the ground, their walls larger and more well-guarded. She began to see people carrying weapons, even while they were tilling fields or herding livestock. She kept well away from them, but whenever she was spotted her powerful vision showed her the angry, frightened looks which came her way. And then, when she was within sight of the mountains, something else appeared.

She was flying slowly, riding a thermal, when the air around her began to feel warmer. The rich tang of wood smoke hit her nostrils. Curiously, she looked around, and soon spotted the source of the smoke: in the distance off to her right, a dark stain marked the sky. Around it, black shapes flew.

The dragon moved on for a little way, but curiosity finally got the better of her. Veering from her current course, she flew toward the smoke. After an hour of two she reached it. A small city, sitting between two rivers, was on fire. On the ground, humans surged in through the city gates and along its streets like ants. Flashes of light burst into life as magical weapons did their work, and she could hear the crashing of ordinary weapons mingling with the screams of the dying.

Above the city, dragons were flying, swooping to breathe fire onto the rooftops and speed up the destruction of the city. Others were outside the walls, diving talons-first onto any human who had managed to escape.

The black dragon watched from a distance, but in a few moments she was spotted. One of the attacking dragons abandoned its assault on a knot of exposed humans, and flew toward her. The black dragon hesitated, but did not retreat, and she and the other dragon began to circle each other warily. The other dragon was male, his scales dark grey.

Have you brought a message? he asked at last. *Did you come from the mountain?*

No, she answered. *I came from the forest. What is this?*

A raid. On the Drachengott's orders. What forest did you come from?

I do not know its name, the black dragon told him. *I was summoned there, but I was attacked and left behind.*

Newly summoned? The other dragon sounded surprised. *Well then, you should go to the mountain and tell the Drachengott that we have destroyed Ritterstadt. He will be pleased, and will give you orders of your own.*

The black dragon listened. *I will go to him,* she said, remembering the dream. She had already seen the place she was going, and she had seen the Drachengott, she was certain of it. The only things she couldn't feel certain about was how — and why.

*

The black dragon continued to know which way she needed to fly, even though she did not know how. She left the burning city behind and returned to the hills, and those led her on to the mountains. Along the way she saw signs of other attacks; the blackened ruins of villages and towns, many of them visibly strewn with bones. The dragon took in the sight of them and wondered why it had happened. She found that she knew some things, but not others. All she had to draw on here was the memory of the night she had been summoned — the vicious anger and hatred that had filled her whole being as she emerged into the world and saw the two humans. They had been the first thing she ever saw, and the first thing she had ever heard was the command from the Jüngen. *Kill them.*

The dragon had not hesitated for an instant. All she knew was that they had summoned her, and that made them her masters. She had been prepared to fight to the death for them, but they had left her to die.

That realisation came back to her slowly, and when it did her anger began to return. It was still with her when she finally reached the valley in the mountains.

It was as it had been in her dream, down to the last detail. The long valley, protected by mountains on both sides, its deep green dotted with human settlements. The dark, brooding clouds above; dragons descending from them to fly alongside her. And the great mountain at the valley's far end —even bigger and more jagged in reality. The black dragon's heartbeat increased at the sight of it. She was nearly there.

She made straight for the mountain, keeping pace with the others, and soon she was close enough to see him for the first time in the waking world.

A dragon so huge that he was one with the mountain. A dragon whose wings could have blotted out the sky. The very air around him and his perch thrummed with energy.

The black dragon began to fly toward him, but then she glanced downward and saw the humans. At least a hundred of them, all gathered at the mountain's foot. A shock of recognition went through her. Unable to stop herself, she flew straight down to them. And there it was: the chunk of granite from her dream. She perched on it, curving white talons gripping the stone, and looked down on the humans as they made their offerings and chanted their prayers to the Drachengott.

The black dragon searched the crowd and quickly spotted her — the woman, her face hard with anger, mouthing the prayers without any sincerity. The dragon could almost feel the hatred coming from her.

Above, the Drachengott's head rose, just as it had in her dream. But now, where the dream had ended, reality moved on. The dragon's long, sharp-snouted head turned, casting a massive shadow over the Jüngen. Any one of them could have drowned in his eyes, which were a deep moss green mixed with gold, shining against the dull grey of his scales. The people and dragons on the ground bowed their heads in reverence rather than meet his gaze.

Only the black dragon did not lower her snout. Her red eyes were fixed on his, and she could not look away. Then the Drachengott spoke.

COME TO ME.

His voice was as big as the mountain he perched on.

The black dragon couldn't resist it. She left her perch and flew to him. The mountain's dark slopes fell away beneath her, and then she was climbing a vast wall of scale — dull, grey scale like the bark of a rotting tree. It heaved massively in time to the giant dragon's breath.

The black dragon felt like an insect beside him. She flew on until she was level with his snout. There, she flapped hard to stay level with him — but then something incredible happened.

The Drachengott breathed out, a slow, deep breath of burning hot air. It should have blown her away, but it didn't. In fact, the moment it touched her, an invisible force took hold of her and she froze in place, hovering with her wings still spread but with no more need to flap. She stayed there, suspended at the end of the Drachengott's snout while his huge eyes examined her. Their expression was impenetrable.

Finally, he spoke, his enormous voice quieter now, but still powerful enough to vibrate in her very bones. *YOU ARE THE ONE.*

Which one am I? she asked, fear spiking through her chest.

YOU ARE THE TRAITOR, his voice rumbled. *YOU ARE SYN.*

Bewildered, the black dragon began to struggle. *No, I—*

YOU WERE MADE TO SERVE MY WORSHIPPERS, he told her, his words unbearable in her ears. *YET YOU DID NOT KILL THE FALLEN ONES. YOU ALLOWED ONE TO ESCAPE. YOU DID NOT PROTECT MY WORSHIPPERS.*

She fought harder, terrified, but the force holding her in place was unbreakable. *How do you know?* she wailed. *How did you know what happened?*

I KNOW ALL, SYN, he said. *YOU HAVE BETRAYED ME.*

I did not!

His eyes bored through her. *YOU HAVE IN YOUR HEART,* he said. *I SEE THE POISON INSIDE. FOR IT, YOU WILL SUFFER. IT IS MY WILL.*

After that, he said nothing more to her. His power dragged her downward, hurling her to the ground, where she landed on her side with an agonising crack.

The Jüngen kept back, but then the Drachengott spoke again, one last time. *TAKE THIS ONE AND PUT HER WITH THE OTHERS FOR PUNISHMENT.*

The black dragon had no chance to fight back. While she lay there, still stunned, the humans pounced on her. They tied her jaws and wings together, and then her legs as well, and three of them carried her away, past others who snarled and spat at the sight of her.

The black dragon was too shocked to resist. Helpless, she looked back at the mountain. She had been summoned, and then condemned.

Why? she thought. *Why?*

Chapter 3

They took the black dragon away from the mountain, down a slope toward a large stone building, grey against green. Armed men let them in, and she was taken down into a dark, gloomy place, where iron cages lined the walls. Inside them, pale, frightened human faces stared out at her, and she heard them whispering.

Her captors took her to an empty cage and threw her inside. The door clanged shut behind her, and then they left. The black dragon lay on her side, unable to get up. Her body ached, and fear paralysed her as thoroughly as the spider venom had. Around her she could hear the human prisoners.

'A dragon? What's a dragon doing here? They never lock them up!'

'I wonder what it did.'

Slowly, the black dragon began to recover her senses. She pulled at the ropes holding her legs and wings together. They wouldn't budge, but her tail was still free. She flicked it, hearing the spikes clatter on the bars. An idea dawned on her, and she shifted her position until she managed to hook the ropes on her forelegs. After a few attempts she got the rope hooked over one of the longer spikes and began to work it back and forth. Her tail spikes were serrated, like her talons, and, though it was painful keeping the right position, the rope frayed and then finally came apart. She hissed triumphantly as she shook her forelegs free, and quickly ripped the rope off her snout with her talons. After that, it was easy enough to free her wings and hind legs.

She got up and shook herself vigorously, then turned her attention to the cage. It was easily big enough for her to move around; she had room to throw herself at the door, which she almost immediately did. But the door wouldn't budge. She pulled and shoved at it, threw her whole weight against it, and finally breathed fire on it.

But nothing worked. The humans around her shrank back as the maddened dragon raged and fought.

This is not fair! she roared. *I am not a traitor! Curse you!*

An image of the Drachengott's dismissive stare returned to her, and she roared again: *Curse you!*

Inevitably, the noise attracted attention. Footsteps came running into the prison, and a Jünger appeared. She was wearing a rich red coat over a fine blue tunic, and she stopped in alarm at the sight of the angry dragon.

The dragon snarled at her. *Let me out of here, or I will burn you!*

The Jünger stood at a safe distance, fingering the red gem around her neck, which was set into a gold amulet. After a moment or two she raised a hand, and sent a beam of pale blue light at the dragon. As it hit her in the throat, freezing cold spiked into her flesh. She fell back, choking, but the sensation faded quickly and she lunged forward, mouth open to spit fire at the woman.

Nothing happened. The dragon roared her frustration and tried again, but her flames would not come. The cold lingered in her throat, locking the flame away inside her.

Coward! she shrieked at the Jünger, who ignored her and quietly left.

Furious, the dragon hurled herself at the cage door again. It still wouldn't give.

Eventually exhausted, she lay down on her belly and rested. The human prisoners began to relax. After a while, one of them crept over to the bars closest to her.

'Why are you here?' he asked.

The dragon looked up at him. He was ragged and weak, and clearly frightened of her. *I am here for no reason, human,* she told him. *I did nothing wrong. Why are* you *here?*

'We disobeyed the Drachengott,' the man said in a hushed voice. 'He gave his commands and we rebelled against them.'

The dragon growled deep in her chest. *I should not be here with you,* she said. *I did not rebel.*

'But you must have done something if you're here,' one of the other prisoners said.

The dragon hissed. *I did nothing!*

The man who had spoken first retreated slightly. 'Do you have a name?' he asked.

The dragon relaxed a little. *I am ... Syn,* she said.

*

Syn kept on trying to escape from her prison, but nothing would give. The door stayed shut, the bars held firm, and her fire did not come back. She fought against it until she ran out of strength, and after that she lay down again and slept. When she woke, the man who had talked to her before was watching.

She looked back at him for a while, then decided to speak to him. *What will they do with us?*

'We're here for punishment,' said the man. 'And when the solstice comes, we will be used as sacrifices to the Drachengott.'

Punishment? Syn repeated.

The man shuddered. 'Yes … You'll find out tomorrow.'

I will not be sacrificed, Syn vowed. *I refuse to die.*

The man looked at the ground. 'I've never heard of a dragon being brought here before,' he said. 'I mean, I thought your kind were different. I didn't even know you *could* rebel.'

Syn cocked her head. *Why is that?*

'Well, you're not like us, are you?' said the man. 'You're closer to the Drachengott than any of us could ever be.'

Because we are the same shape? Syn suggested.

The man looked up, his expression puzzled. 'Don't you know?'

No, Syn said bluntly. *I was summoned by two Jüngen not long ago. I know nothing about the Drachengott.*

'He made the world,' the man said. 'He created humankind. But some people rebelled — the Gottlosen. We are the ones who came back to him, to find redemption. Now Jüngen like us serve him: we're fighting a way to wipe out the Gottlosen and reclaim the lands they took in the Drachengott's name.'

And us? said Syn. *Dragons?*

'You came from him,' said the man. 'All dragons are part of him. Fragments of himself. He never leaves the sacred mountain, so he made your kind to work for him and to serve beside us. That's why I can't imagine a dragon ever turning against him.'

Syn listened, bewildered. *I am part of him?*

'Yes,' said the man. 'You all are.'

Syn lay still, contemplating what the prisoner had told her. She was part of the Drachengott. Made in his image. And yet he had turned his back on her. Called her a traitor and sent her to this place. And all for reasons which made no sense to her.

Despair and bewilderment replaced her anger. *I do not understand …*

'It's hard to obey,' said the man. 'I tried, but …'

Syn looked up at him. *What is your name?*

'I am Franz,' he said.

Syn looked away again. *I think we have both been betrayed, Franz.*

*

The next day came, and Syn learned what Franz had meant by 'punishment'. It began early in the morning, when she and the rest of the prisoners were alerted by the sound of footsteps. Syn had been asleep, but when she woke up she found the others already awake. To a man and woman, they had huddled against the rear bars of their cages. Some were sobbing quietly, and most had gone pale.

Syn watched, wondering what they were so afraid of. She didn't have to wonder for long.

The woman who had taken her fire away the day before came in, and the other prisoners flinched at the sight of her. Syn snarled. The woman stared back at her, expressionless. Then she raised a hand—

Pain shot through Syn's body; burning, agonising pain. It felt as though her scales, talons and teeth were all being torn out. She collapsed, screaming, only dimly aware of the human prisoners writhing along with her.

Then, unbelievably, the pain intensified. Syn thrashed on the floor of her cage, unable to even cry out. Blackness started to close over her eyes, flashing red in time to her heartbeat.

But she did not black out. Suddenly, the pain vanished, leaving her gasping. She lay on her side, jaws hanging open, her wings limp. Above the roaring in her ears, she could hear the humans groaning and crying out. But it was over.

For now.

*

That first bout of torture was not the end of what Syn suffered in the prison — not by a long way. Every day — sometimes twice in one day — the Jünger would come back and, without a word, cast the pain spell on them all. No routine, no reasons given. Only pain, day after day.

It was enough to kill two of the human prisoners, and Syn watched their bodies being dragged away. By now she was too weak herself to make any real effort to escape. All she had was thought. Lying in her cage, eyes blank, she let her mind work. Beyond vague notions of freedom, all she could think of was the Drachengott.

She was a part of him, and he had rejected her — and for what? For nothing. She had done nothing. And yet here she was, suffering because of him. And soon she could die, when she had barely begun to live.

It was an image that would not leave her. It flashed across her mind while the pain ripped at her. It ran through her dreams and filled her mind when she was awake. The Dragon God, condemning her to this. And the more she thought of it, the more her hatred grew. It was all she had to cling to in that place. Hatred and anger. She screamed it out during the torture — sometimes aloud, sometimes only in her head. *Curse him! Curse him!* It kept her alive, kept her sane. Within a few days, it had become her obsession.

And then, one night, her chance came at last.

*

Syn was asleep when the familiar, dreaded sound of footsteps woke her up. She got up immediately, tail lashing, and fear chewing at her insides.

But this time it was different. The footsteps grew louder, and multiplied, and, as the human prisoners started up in fright and confusion, a dozen people came running into the prison. Syn drew back, hissing, but the intruders ignored her. They split up and went to the human cages. Metal clanged, and the doors came open. The human prisoners emerged, all talking at once.

'What's going on?'

'Who are—?'

One of their rescuers held up a hand. 'Quiet — there's no time. We have to get out of here, now.'

Syn went to the bars of her own cage, nostrils flaring. She knew that scent. *You are the angry one from the mountain,* she said softly.

The woman turned toward her. 'You,' she said. 'I remember you: you're the one—'

Syn shoved at her cage door. *Let me out — you must let me out of this place!*

The woman's expression hardened. 'I don't think so, dragon. I know too much about your kind.' She turned to leave, waving at the others to follow, but the man named Franz stopped her.

'Wait,' he said. 'We should let her go. She hates the Drachengott as much as we do.'

'She's still a part of him,' said the woman. 'If we take her with us—'

'We don't have to,' said Franz. 'We let her out and she'll attack the guards — give us time to escape.'

'Would you?' The woman looked at Syn.

I will not go with you, said Syn. *I will have my revenge here. Only set me free.*

The woman nodded once, then waved to her friends. 'Go. Leave me to take care of this.'

The others hurried out of the prison, some supported by their friends. Only the woman stayed behind. Syn could see the red gemstone glinting around her neck. The woman raised a hand, and the freezing sensation in Syn's throat went away.

Syn spat a small flame, and looked up gratefully at the woman. *How did you do that?*

'Magic can do anything if you have the strength for it,' said the woman. She made another gesture and the cage door came open. Syn stepped out, talons clicking on the floor. *Thank you, human.*

The woman had already made a move to leave, but she paused and looked back. 'What's your name?'

I am Syn. And you?

'Tanja,' said the woman. 'Good luck, Syn.'

And to you, Tanja.

Tanja ran away up the stairs, and Syn followed her, emerging into the corridor above in time to see the woman running away ahead of her, pursued by a squad of armed men who were emerging from a side door.

Wasting no time, Syn drew a deep breath and sent a plume of silver fire down the corridor. The guards screamed as it enveloped them. Those closest to the dragon died instantly; those furthest away writhed on the ground, skin and clothes burning.

Only Tanja was far enough away to avoid the fire. She ducked through the doorway at the far end of the corridor and fled into the night after her friends.

Syn didn't pause over her victims. She surged forward, trampling the bodies in her way, and the moment she was out in the open she launched herself into the air. Her wings ached from lack of use, and she wobbled a little, but she recovered quickly enough, soaring up and over the prison building like a great black bat.

Free!

Ecstasy filled her. But anger quickly followed. She wheeled around, moonlight shining on her scales, and flew straight back toward the Drachengott's mountain. The moon sat behind it, outlining its massive shape. She could see the hunched back of the Drachengott himself; the curves of his great neck and folded wings.

Hatred burned in Syn's chest at the sight. She flew closer, so intent on her goal that she didn't see the other dragon coming until it was too late.

A dark shape came rushing out of the gloom and hit her side-on. She felt the talons slash through her hide, and then she was falling, tumbling sideways with her wings flailing. Before she could recover, the other dragon was on her. Teeth sank into her wing, and, as she struggled to break free, several other dragons arrived to join in the attack. Talons and teeth ripped at her from every side, and as the first dragon let go of her wing a flurry of brutal blows sent her plummeting toward the ground.

She fell, head-first, her damaged wings refusing to save her, while above the other dragons chanted, a horrible, mocking sound. *Syn! Syn! Syn!*

They didn't come after her — not immediately. But at any moment one or more of them would surely descend on her and finish her off. With a last, desperate effort, Syn wrenched her wings forward. They caught the air, and she pulled out of her dive and began to fly as she had never flown before, away from the valley and the mountain, as fast as she could go.

The other dragons chased her — she could feel the wind of their wings, and the jaws ripping at her tail. But Syn did not let them catch her. She flew on, feeling no pain, until the lesser mountains which edged the valley passed below her and she was over forest again. When they reached the edge of the valley, as if acting on some unheard signal, the dragons suddenly turned back and let her go.

Syn did not stop, even though exhaustion and weakness closed over her mind and body, and she had to force herself to go on. Ahead of her there was nothing but wilderness — forest like the one where she had first been summoned, broken up by small rocky glens and other secret places. *Good places to hide*, she thought vaguely.

With that, her wings started to let her drift downward, almost of their own accord. Spotting a large tree, she made a clumsy landing in its upper branches.

She stayed there for a long time, half collapsed over a large bough, while the shock slowly sank in. Her temporary immunity to pain had worn off, and now she could feel her injuries all too well. Her back and sides were slashed open, her right wing damaged, and one of her hind legs had been torn just behind the heel and wouldn't move properly. She could feel the blood trickling down her sides and dropping steadily onto the leaves and branches around her, pattering softly like rain.

All her strength seemed to be draining away with it.

But I will not die, she thought. *No! I cannot; I will not. I will live. And I will make those who have done this to me suffer — I swear it.*

With that thought she sank into unconsciousness, and dreamed again.

*

This dream was as vivid as the first — more so, in fact. The colours were brighter than anything in the real world, almost lurid, with a yellow light haloing everything in sight.

She drifted through time and across strange landscapes, and finally onto an ashy wasteland where five people stood. Four of the five carried weapons unlike anything she had ever seen before. They wore armour, and their faces were etched with experience. They turned to face the fifth human, whose face Syn could not see.

'Well,' one of them said, 'we're here at last, and we have what we need. Finally, we can defeat him.'

'And it's all thanks to you,' said another, the youngest of the group, whose face Syn knew. He smiled at the fifth. 'I just wish you would tell us who you really are.'

The fifth figure said nothing, but at that moment she looked up, and stared straight at Syn. She smiled as though she could see Syn's shock of recognition — and the dream vanished in a flash of red light.

*

Syn woke up, her heart still pounding. Morning had come, and her wounds had started to mend. Her whole body had stiffened, and she could barely move. But none of that mattered now. She was alive, and she had seen ...

As the dream slowly soaked through her mind, everything opened up before her. She knew what she must do now, and she silently made a vow.

I will wait until I am healed, and then I will leave this place. I will learn about magic, and I will master it. And then ... then I will do everything in my power to make that dream become real. Her red eyes narrowed. *And once I am ready, I know exactly where I must go — and who I will find first.*

Chapter 4

Dawn. Rutger got out of bed quietly in the semi-darkness. An icy chill filled the air, even indoors, and he took a set of thick furs down off their hook and pulled them on as quickly as he could. The soft rabbit fur inside the coat brushed against his arms, and he shivered pleasantly as he stepped around the beds where his two unmarried brothers were lying, still asleep.

He picked up his sword from where it lent against the wall by the door, buckled it on and slipped out of the house. Outside, everything was black and white. Snow covered the ground and rooftops of the village, blinding under the pale sky. It had caked the logs of the stockade, and beyond them even the Schwartz Forest looked white.

In a pen nearby, a couple of deer huffed clouds of steam. Rutger stopped to pat one on the nose, and then walked off toward the stockade, boots crunching on the snow. The gates were closed at this hour, but the night watchmen were still there, blinking sleepily in the stark light. Rutger waved to them, and the nearest looked down from his perch.

'*Guten Morgen*,' he said through a yawn. 'Off to waste more time, are you?'

'I have to check my traps,' Rutger replied stiffly.

The guard chuckled. 'Come on, everyone knows what you get up to out there every morning. You didn't bribe the blacksmith to make you that sword just so you could cut wood with it.'

'It's for protection,' said Rutger. 'Will you just open the gates now?'

'Oh, fine.' The guard waved to his colleague and the two of them hauled on a pair of ropes attached to pulleys. The gates slowly creaked open, pushing up twin embankments of snow, and Rutger gratefully walked through into the open. But as he set out for the forest, he heard the second guard mutter: 'Obsessive fool. Ten years and he still won't let it go. No wonder he's never found a wife.'

Rutger didn't look back, but his mouth tightened. He crossed the snowfield outside the village and entered the forest, green eyes focused determinedly forward as an icy breeze stirred through his dark brown hair.

In winter, the place where Horst had died looked dead as well, all colour bleached out of it so that the trees were bones. There was a deep stillness between the trees.

Rutger hadn't lied. He set out on his usual route, checking the traps he had set the day before. The hunting was never as good at this time of year, but he had caught a couple of weasels, a rabbit, and a couple of precious mink — all wearing their white winter coats, which would make them more valuable to the buyers further west, where he sent a portion of the furs he gathered every year.

He tied the dead animals to his belt, just as Horst had once done — but as always his route took him back to the same place it did every day.

The clearing hadn't changed much, even after ten years. By now the burnt trees had mostly recovered, although two or three had died and now stood bare and grim against the pale sky. The hanging bodies were long gone, and, since for some reason the Jüngen had never returned, no more had replaced them.

Rutger felt the familiar stab of fear as he entered the clearing, but it faded quickly, and was replaced with confidence. The Jüngen and the spiders were gone. This was his place now.

He untied the string of dead animals from his waist and carefully hung it from a branch. Then he drew his sword. It was a plain weapon — old Helmut the blacksmith normally made ploughshares and shovels, not weapons. But, in exchange for a fine mink coat for his wife, Helmut had put together a basic blade. He had even welded on a cross-guard. And — this was the thing about it that Rutger liked best — the handgrip had been carved out of the broken dragon horn, which was the only souvenir left from that terrible night. Helmut had sanded and polished it, and the horn felt beautifully smooth against Rutger's callused palm.

He took a deep breath, placed his feet fell apart, and began. He had never had any kind of formal training, as there were no real fighters in the village. While there were plenty of people who could handle a bow, there were no swordsmen. All Rutger could do was practise the moves he had worked out for himself over the years. He swung the sword one-handed, striking the air from several different angles to warm up. Then he turned his attention to one of the dead trees, which he had dubbed the practice tree. It was already covered in cuts and gouges which had removed large sections of bark.

Rutger attacked the practice tree once again, twisting and darting around it as if it were alive. He blocked imaginary blows, stabbed and slashed, and finally cut off one of the few remaining lower branches.

As he stopped to rest, the guard's remark came back to him and he suddenly started to feel stupid. He looked around the clearing, memories flashing across his mind, and as always they twisted the sense of humiliation into anger. It was the very reason he chose to practise here. He closed his eyes, forcing himself to relive what had happened here. The Jüngen, faces full of cold contempt. The foul stench of the hanging corpses. The screeching roar of the dragon as it launched itself across the clearing with its teeth bared.

And Horst. Horst fighting back with impossible courage, fighting to defend him. Horst dying, and Rutger there, unable to save him.

Rage coursed through him, and he opened his eyes and launched himself at the tree. But it wasn't a tree now. It was a Jünger. It was the dragon who had killed Horst. It was all of them — every single one of those murdering scum, and the monstrous god they obeyed. Everything he hated, all rolled together into one.

Eventually, exhausted, he slumped down on a rock to catch his breath. His arms and chest ached, and he was sweating inside his furs. He pulled his gloves off and rubbed some snow over his face, then rolled some more into a lump and chewed on it, shuddering as the ice made his teeth tingle.

After a while, the back of his neck prickled, and he became slowly aware that he was being watched. Snatching up the sword, he got to his feet. 'Who's there?'

There was silence for a moment, and then a voice answered.

'Hello.'

As the voice spoke, its owner stepped out from behind a tree, and Rutger started in surprise. The stranger was a woman about his own age, wearing a long coat of silvery wolf fur. Her hair was lustrous black, and her face very pale, and although she looked strange she was the most beautiful woman Rutger had ever seen. She could have been a rich noblewoman stepping out of her palace — she could never have looked at home out here in the forest. This was the kind of woman who belonged in perfumed gardens and banqueting halls full of fine tapestries and golden goblets. Her face was fine-boned and intelligent, her eyes large and bright, her every movement graceful and poised. Even the fur coat managed to look like a velvet gown as it clung to her elegant figure.

Rutger's mouth went dry. 'Who are you?' he managed to ask.

The woman smiled. 'My name is Swanhild. And you?'

'Uh ... Rutger.' He lowered the sword. 'How did you get here? You're not from my village.'

Swanhild cocked her head. 'Which village is that, Rutger?'

'It's called Gothendorf,' he said with some effort. Talking had suddenly become a lot harder.

'Gothendorf,' Swanhild repeated. Her voice was soft and musical, and it made the name of his home village sound almost poetic.

'Yes, that's it,' Rutger said stupidly. 'Where are you from?'

'I don't have a home,' said Swanhild. 'It was destroyed long ago.' She came toward him, making his heart beat faster, but stopped at the practice tree and ran a long, delicate hand over the cuts in its trunk. 'Were you practising here to protect your own home?' she asked.

'Yes, I suppose so.' Rutger felt himself blushing. 'Did you see me?'

'Yes, I did,' said Swanhild. 'I wondered why you were out here practising alone. Does no one want to learn with you?'

Rutger shifted uneasily. 'No ... not really.'

'Why not? And even if you must work alone, why here? Are you hiding from something? Is swordplay forbidden in Gothendorf?'

'It's not forbidden,' said Rutger. 'I came here because … It's a special place here.'

Swanhild paused, her hand still on the tree. 'Why is that? Can you tell me?'

Rutger suddenly didn't want to look at her anymore. He turned away, staring vacantly at the trees of the clearing. 'My brother died here,' he said. 'It was a long time ago, but … I was there. I was only a boy — I couldn't save him.'

'I'm sorry,' Swanhild said softly. 'How did he die?'

'He was murdered by Jüngen,' said Rutger. Even now, talking about it upset him. He started to pace around, his sword hanging at his side. 'We stumbled across them here … They attacked us. Horst — he died saving me. If only I—'

Swanhild came closer. 'Don't blame yourself,' she said. 'You were only a boy. And those Jüngen had a weapon you could never have fought against: magic.'

Rutger stopped pacing and thrust the sword into the snowy ground. 'It's not good enough,' he said, with a touch of desperation. 'There has to be something I can do. It's only a matter of time before the Jüngen armies break through the fortified cities in Drucht Valley and start attacking here as well. Everyone at home pretends it won't ever happen, but it will. I know it will. I have to do something.'

Swanhild nodded slowly. 'You are a brave man, Rutger. And perhaps …'

He calmed down and looked at her properly again. Her beauty stunned him. 'Why did you come here?' he asked. 'Are you looking for shelter? Are you lost?'

'I was looking for someone,' said Swanhild. 'Someone I have been searching for a long time. But now … I think I may have found him.'

'Me?' Rutger said blankly.

'Yes.' Swanhild turned away to study the practice tree. After a moment's contemplation, she raised a hand and shot a bolt of silver light from her palm. It hit the tree, which instantly disintegrated into a heap of ash on the snow.

Rutger gasped. 'How did—?'

Swanhild turned toward him. 'Magic, of course.'

He backed away from her. 'But only Jüngen can use magic! You're not … ?'

'No, I'm not a Jünger,' said Swanhild. 'I learned what I know from others. Rebels who turned their backs on the Drachengott, but who can still use the powers he gave them.' She smiled. 'You see, the truth is that anyone can use magic if they only know how. And if you want to fight back against the Jüngen, well … perhaps you can learn.'

Rutger's face darkened. 'Decent people should never learn magic — it's evil.'

'It's a tool,' said Swanhild. 'That's all.' She indicated the sword in his hand. 'Your sword can be used to murder people, or protect them. The difference is how you choose to use it. Magic is the same.'

'A sword can't destroy entire cities,' said Rutger.

'True,' said Swanhild. 'Yes, very true.' She held out a hand, and a silvery flame flickered into life on her palm. It sat there, just above her skin, burning without fuel. Rutger stared at it, both fascinated and repelled.

'I should tell you the truth about why I'm here,' said Swanhild. 'You see, I was with the rebels for ten years after I lost my home. Eventually they came to trust me enough to teach me their skills. But we argued. I wanted to recruit others — ordinary people who had never worshipped the Drachengott — and train them as well. Build an army, so we could take on the Jüngen. But the rebels refused to share their power, and after I argued with them once too often they tried to have me locked up. I was forced to go into exile. But my opinions haven't changed.'

Rutger kept staring at the flame, and at her. 'You could teach me how to do that?'

Swanhild paused. 'I have to be very careful. As you say, magic is dangerous. It should never be given to anyone lightly.'

Rutger's heart had already started to pound. He could smell her now — a sweet, flowery scent that made his head spin. The magical flame balanced on her palm mesmerised him. Magic. The power to destroy a tree as thick as his whole body with a single gesture. The Jüngen had used it to lay waste to entire cities, but now that power was there in front of him, almost within his reach. His mouth went dry.

'Would you teach me?' he asked.

Swanhild smiled at him. She closed her fist, and the flame disappeared. 'How would you use it if I did?'

'To defend my village,' said Rutger.

'But your people would be afraid of you,' said Swanhild. 'They wouldn't welcome your help. They might even banish you.'

Rutger bit his lip. 'Then ... then I'd use it to fight back against the Jüngen, and defend my people that way.'

'You wouldn't misuse it?'

'Never,' said Rutger. He looked hopefully at Swanhild.

'Perhaps we should talk some more,' she said after a pause. 'It's been a long journey and I'm tired. You should go back to your home now.'

'Come with me,' said Rutger. 'You can stay in my house.'

Swanhild shook her head. 'It would be too dangerous,' she said. 'A magic user would never be welcome, and especially not one who had associated with Jüngen. You must keep me a secret, Rutger — even from your own family.'

'But you can't stay out here,' he said.

'Oh, I can,' said Swanhild, smiling again. 'Don't worry about me. Come back here tomorrow if you want to see me again.'

Reluctantly, Rutger put his sword back in his belt. 'You're right, I should go. I have work to do.'

'Go, then,' said Swanhild. 'It was good to meet you — I enjoyed talking with you.'

Rutger took the string of carcasses down from the tree, and tied it around his waist. 'It was ... good to talk with you as well,' he said, feeling stupid again. His whole body felt thick and clumsy, and he fumbled with the string as he re-tied it. He made a desperate effort not to ask the next question, but he couldn't stop himself. As he started to walk away, he stopped and looked back at Swanhild, who stood out against the snow with her silver furs and glossy black hair. 'Will you still be here tomorrow? You won't ... leave, will you?'

She smiled again. 'Don't you trust me?'

'I don't really know you.'

'That's fair,' said Swanhild. 'But don't worry – I'll be here.'

Rutger left, face burning. This time he managed not to look back. And that was why he did not see the gleam of satisfaction in Swanhild's strange eyes.

Chapter 5

Rutger couldn't concentrate for the rest of the day. He went back to the village and to his workshop, where his younger brother Gerhart helped him skin the animals he had caught. Rutger left Gerhart to begin the skinning, while he turned his attention to the other furs which were now ready. He had been working on a fine white mink wrap — a special order from a customer all the way over in Hundsburg, which he had never visited. The stitching had to be as neat as possible. But, even though this was a job he had done a hundred times before, he kept jabbing himself with the needle. His body might have returned to his small, leather-smelling workshop, but his mind was back in the clearing with Swanhild. She was unlike any woman he had ever met before, and what she had offered ...

'Are you all right?' Gerhart asked, after Rutger had jammed the needle under his fingernail and broken into a stream of swear words.

Rutger wiped the blood off his finger onto his apron. 'I'm fine. How are those hides coming along?'

'I've nearly finished scraping them.' Gerhart, small and blond with a freckled face, peered at his brother. 'You look as though you have something on your mind.'

'I'm just hoping I can finish this wrap in time,' said Rutger. 'Did the lining arrive yet?'

'Yes, it's over there,' said Gerhart. He paused. 'You were gone for a long time this morning. Did anything happen in the forest?'

An image of Swanhild's face shot to the front of Rutger's mind. 'No,' he lied. 'No, nothing happened. Pass me the thread, will you?'

In spite of his distraction, Rutger managed to finish sewing the last of the pelts together, and made a start on attaching the silky cloth lining he had bought from Adwala, the weaver next door. But while he worked, all he could think of was Swanhild — and before long he had started to worry. What if she wasn't there the next day after all? What if she decided he wasn't worth her time and moved on to find someone else to train? After all, she had never said she was going to train him, and why would she? He was nobody; just a furrier who played at swords. He had never done anything important with his life, and most likely he never would. All of these wild ideas about learning to be a warrior were just that: wild ideas which couldn't possibly lead to anything. No doubt Swanhild had only said what she had said to get rid of him; by now she would be long gone, and he would never see her again.

It was enough to make him want to leave now, and go running back to the clearing to find her. He had to fight off the urge, but even so it put him in a low mood for the whole evening. He kept snapping at Gerhart without really meaning to, and his brother was in a sulk by the time they finished work for the day.

The home they shared backed onto the workshop, and by the time they arrived home, Rocco had the dinner ready. He was the one of

Rutger's four surviving brothers, but, since he had never found a wife or shown any interest in finding one, he still lived with Rutger and Gerhart, who at thirteen was too young to marry.

Today, Rocco had brought back a fine loaf of bread and an apple cake for each of them. 'I made them myself,' he said proudly, as Rutger and Gerhart joined him at the table.

Rutger helped himself to a slice of bread. 'How was the bakery today?' he asked automatically.

'Just as usual,' said Rocco. 'How were the mink?'

'Smelly,' said Gerhart, which made his brother laugh.

Rutger didn't join in the laughter. He spread cream cheese on the bread and ate it without really tasting it. After today's strange encounter, normal life felt irrelevant.

'So,' said Rocco, 'how was your swordplay this morning, Rut?'

Rutger started. 'Uh ... it was fine. Actually,' he added with a touch of recklessness, 'I destroyed the practice tree today.'

'Really?' said Gerhart. 'You mean you cut it down?'

'Yes,' Rutger lied. 'Hit it one time too many at last.'

'You should have brought some back – we could have used the firewood,' said Rocco. He grinned to himself. 'If you finally killed the tree, does that mean you're a swordmaster now?'

Rutger chuckled. 'Surely.'

Gerhart looked slightly worried all of a sudden. 'You're not going to leave, are you?' he asked.

Rutger stared at him. 'What? What gave you that idea?'

'It's just ... you were acting so strange today,' said Gerhart. 'And I always thought you might leave anyway.'

'What for?' said Rutger, bewildered.

'Because you're angry,' said Gerhart. 'You're always angry, deep down. You've been that way as long as I can remember. And you practise with your sword every day. So I thought, once you were ready, you would go east and fight the Jüngen.'

Rutger did not know what to say. He looked at Gerhart in astonishment, then at Rocco. He half expected Rocco to say something — tell Gerhart he was being fanciful. But Rocco's expression said he agreed with Gerhart.

'You didn't think I was going to do that, did you?' Rutger asked him, still not quite able to believe what Gerhart had just said.

'Well, *everyone* thinks that, really,' said Rocco.

'They do?'

'Yes,' said Rocco. 'I know nobody talks about it, but it's just ... everyone knows. One day Rutger is going to leave his business for Gerhart to take over, and leave Gothendorf to become a soldier. Why else would he have that sword and practise with it every day, if he didn't want to do that? I mean, that *is* what you are planning to do, isn't it?'

'I ... I don't know,' Rutger admitted.

'I think it's what you want to do, though,' said Rocco. 'Even if you don't realise it.'

Rutger took another piece of bread, and ate it slowly while he tried to think. Had everyone really been thinking that? Had the whole village been waiting all this time, expecting him to pack up and leave at any moment?

He noticed the anxious look Gerhart was giving him, and quickly shook his head. 'No. I'm not going to leave.'

Gerhart didn't look convinced. 'Then why do you practise with your sword all the time?'

'So I can be ready if we are ever attacked, of course,' said Rutger. 'That's all.'

'You should learn archery, then,' said Rocco. 'It's far more useful against dragons.'

'When I fought a dragon, it was on the ground,' said Rutger, and left it at that.

*

Rutger couldn't sleep that night, and the night itself seemed to last forever. He lay and stared at the wood-beamed ceiling, listening to Rocco's faint snoring and the rustle of blankets as Gerhart turned over in bed. Their words kept repeating themselves in his head. *You're not going to leave, are you? It's what you want to do.*

When he finally did go to sleep, he dreamed of Horst. The two of them were together in the clearing, and the black dragon hung in the air over their heads, frozen in time with its mouth open in a silent roar. Rutger's workbench was there, and he and Horst were busy skinning mink together, just as they had done in the old days when Rutger's workshop still belonged to his older brother. Neither one of them spoke. They worked together in companionable silence, hanging each fresh pelt from a tree until the clearing was red with them. But the hill behind the clearing soon began to draw Rutger's attention. He kept looking at it when he left the bench to hang up another pelt. In all the years that had passed, he had never been beyond that hill — never seen what lay on the other side. Sometimes he had dreamed of going beyond it, although what he found was always different. Sometimes there was a huge, glittering city there. Sometimes there was the sea. And sometimes there was only more forest, its snowy floor thick with skinned mink and the bones of murdered men.

But this time, when Rutger's dream self wandered away out of the clearing, he found someone waiting for him. Swanhild, standing with her back to him and looking out over a landscape unlike anything he had ever seen before.

What is it? he asked.

She turned to smile at him. *It's the world.*

*

Dawn light woke him up, just as usual — a thin beam of it shining on his face through a shutter which he always left ajar on purpose. He lay in bed for a while, too warm and comfortable to want to leave it, but then the memory of the previous day came rushing back and he leapt out from under the covers. He snatched up his clothes and pulled them on with careless haste, not bothering to keep quiet this time, and made for the door before he had even finished fastening his coat. He was in such a hurry that he nearly forgot his sword, but he stopped and darted back for it.

While he was buckling it on, he glanced over at Gerhart's bed and saw that his brother's eyes were open and fixed on him. They were blue, and solemn.

'Sorry, I didn't mean to wake you,' Rutger whispered. 'Go back to sleep.'

'It's all right if you leave, Rutger,' Gerhart said as Rutger turned away.

Rutger stopped. 'I told you I'm not going.'

'But when you do, it's all right,' said Gerhart. 'Just promise you'll come back.'

Rutger smiled at him. 'Don't be silly. I'll always come back. Now you go back to sleep — I'm just going to check the traps.'

He left the house, hand on his sword hilt. But the instant he had closed the door behind him, he dropped the pretence and broke into a run. Slipping on the fresh snow that had fallen during the night, he bolted for the gate. The same two guards were on duty, and they snickered as Rutger stumbled to a halt.

'In a rush today, Swordmaster Rutger?' one asked.

'Obviously yes,' said Rutger, too worried to rise to the bait. 'Open the gates.'

The guard shrugged and waved to his friend, and the gates creaked open.

Rutger hurried out through them, forcing himself to slow down. Falling over wouldn't get him back to the clearing any faster. Even so, he heard one of the guards say, 'What's he in such a hurry for? The trees aren't going to run away.'

Rutger laughed weakly at the idea as he entered the forest. It looked just the same as it had the day before, but this time he didn't check his traps at all. He made straight for the clearing, hood pulled up against the cold, his doubts whispering to him that he was wasting his time. What was the point in hurrying? She wouldn't be there.

But if she wasn't, he thought suddenly, he wouldn't let her go. He would search the forest until he found her, and he would beg her to teach him. He *had* to learn how to use magic, and without her there would never be another chance for him. He wouldn't let this chance go.

As he came closer to the clearing, he saw something that made his heart shoot into his mouth. Something big and dark against the snow, nestled amongst the trees as if it had always been there. He recognised the shape immediately, but couldn't quite believe it, even when he had entered the clearing and seen it properly.

There was a house in the clearing now. Not a proper one, he saw now — more of a hut, with a roof of wooden planks and a rough doorway covered by a curtain. Out the front a fire was burning. A silver fire, without fuel, which had melted a large patch of snow away and dried the ground underneath. A couple of logs had been put on either side of it to serve as seats, and one was already occupied.

'Swanhild!' Rutger strode toward her, relief warming him just as well as the fire.

She looked up at him with a smile. 'So you're back. But you look as though you thought I wouldn't be here. Did you think I lied to you?'

Rutger laughed as he sat down on the other side of the fire. 'I thought you might change your mind about me.'

'You didn't even know if I had made up my mind in the first place, did you?' she asked mischievously. 'What if I had decided to leave you, and *then* changed my mind?'

'Then that would have been a good change of mind,' said Rutger. 'But I'm ...' he looked down shyly. 'I'm so glad you stayed.'

'Thank you,' said Swanhild. 'It's good to be welcome. How do you like my camp?' she added, indicating the hut.

'Camp?' said Rutger. 'It's a house!'

'Only the shell of one,' said Swanhild. 'I haven't had time to put much inside it yet. And I won't unless I have to. I just thought it would be best to have a proper shelter in all this snow.'

'You used magic, didn't you?' said Rutger. 'Those dead trees are all gone.'

'Yes, I pulled them apart and used them to build,' said Swanhild. 'And what about you?' she added. 'Have you come to practise with your sword again?'

'No,' said Rutger. 'There's no point. You're right: against magic, swords are useless. I've been wasting my time all these years.' He drew the sword and tossed it down at his feet.

'Not useless,' said Swanhild. 'No, not useless at all. Most Jüngen only know the most basic magic — your sword could deal with them easily enough. And besides, physical strength makes your ability to contain and control magic much greater.'

Rutger's heart beat faster. 'Then will you teach me?' he asked. 'Have you decided?'

'Yes, I have,' she said. 'I spent last night thinking it over. In my life I have learned to follow my instincts, and my instincts tell me I should teach you.'

Rutger breathed deeply to keep himself calm. 'Then you'll show me magic?'

'Yes,' said Swanhild. 'At first I'll teach you basic magic — nothing too powerful. If you have an aptitude for it, and demonstrate that you can be trusted to use it wisely, we can move on from there.'

'Thank you!' said Rutger. 'Oh, thank you. I promise I'll be careful.'

Swanhild nodded with a smile. 'Then let's begin today.'

Chapter 6

Their first lesson began simply enough. Rutger sat on his log and listened closely, while Swanhild explained the basics of how magic worked.

'Energy is everywhere around us,' she said. 'It makes the sun hot and the snow cold. It makes a heart beat and a tree grow. But when that energy is channelled and controlled by a living creature, it becomes known as magic. The more energy you can control, the more powerful your magic. How much you can handle is determined by two things: strength and willpower. And by "strength" I don't just mean physical strength, although you're strong enough. There is inner strength as well: how robust your heart and bones are, how well you can resist poison and disease. A man may look weak but be stronger than he seems. And next we have willpower — strength in the mind, the ability to concentrate. By being physically strong you can contain plenty of magical energy, but you won't be able to control it without a strong mind. Does all this make sense so far?'

Rutger nodded. 'So you have to be intelligent?'

'No,' said Swanhild. 'In fact intelligence can sometimes make it more difficult — a stupid person can be much better at staying focused, because they have fewer thoughts to distract them!' She laughed.

Rutger laughed as well. 'That's true. I should be safe, then.'

'Oh, I wouldn't call you stupid,' said Swanhild.

'But I'm not too smart either,' said Rutger. 'I mean, I'm only a furrier. I don't even know how to read.'

Swanhild shrugged. 'I've met clever farmers and stupid scholars. Your skills and station in life don't change your inner worth. But now, let's continue.'

Rutger smiled bashfully. 'That's kind of you.'

Swanhild smiled back. 'So now you understand the most important principals of magic,' she said. 'But there's more to it. If there weren't, anyone could use magic without needing to be taught. However, before anyone can begin, the ability has to be unlocked. Until now this was a secret which even the Jüngen never talked about. They believe that only the Drachengott himself can unlock the gift of magic. But that's a lie. Any magic user can do it for anyone else they choose, if they know how to do it. Today, I will do it for you.'

'How?' asked Rutger. 'Will you cast a spell on me?'

'No,' said Swanhild. 'What you need ... is this.' She reached into the leather pouch that hung from her waist, and brought out a gemstone about the size of a baby's fist. She gently tossed it over the fire to Rutger, who caught it and turned it over in his fingers. It was a blue stone, its surface perfectly smooth. When he held it up to the light he could see straight into its perfect, sky-coloured depths.

'It's beautiful,' he said 'What do I do with it?'

'It's a sapphire,' said Swanhild, 'which I pulled out of the earth myself. All gemstones have energy locked inside them — remnants of the original magic which made the world. Every magic user needs one.'

'Is that why the Jüngen wear those stones around their necks?' asked Rutger, remembering the two he had seen in the clearing that night.

'No,' said Swanhild. 'The Jüngen' necklaces are fakes. Only for show. If they were real, anyone could steal one. Many have, hoping to claim the Drachengott's power for themselves. But the necklaces do nothing; they are only status symbols. Bought and sold. The real power is inside.'

'Inside?' Rutger repeated.

'Yes.' Swanhild made a gesture, and the sapphire gently lifted itself out of Rutger's hand and returned to hers. 'To unlock magic in you, I will have to put this stone inside you.'

Rutger blanched. 'You're joking.'

Swanhild silently pulled her furs open and showed him the upper part of her chest. There, just above her breasts, a deep scar stood out against her pale skin. 'The process is not painless,' she said, 'but it only takes a moment. Afterward, the gemstone will be a part of you: it will sit inside your ribcage and draw magic out of the world around you, storing it ready for you to use whenever you want to. Every Jünger has had this done.'

Rutger rubbed a hand over his forehead; he had started to sweat. 'I can't believe— This is mad. You honestly want to put that rock in me?'

'No,' said Swanhild. 'It's not a question of what I want. What matters is what *you* want. If you want to use magic, say so and I'll unlock the gift. If not, say so and we can end it here.'

He hesitated. 'How much would it hurt?'

'Pain is temporary,' said Swanhild. 'As I said, it would be quick. The initiation is very painful for Jüngen — they make it that way because they believe it is a necessary trial. But I don't believe that, so I would make it as painless as possible.'

'Would it hurt afterwards? Would I be able to feel it in there?'

'Yes, you would,' said Swanhild. 'But it would hurt only if you used too much magic at once. When I use my own magic, I can feel my gemstone; it ... pulsates, I suppose. But if I try to use too much magic in one go, it burns. It is a warning to me to stop, and that makes it a good thing. You understand?'

Rutger nodded slowly. 'Pain tells you when you are hurting yourself.'

'Just that,' said Swanhild. She put the gemstone away. 'Take your time to think about it: this isn't a decision to be made hastily.'

Rutger stared at the fire. 'I want you to do it,' he said after a moment.

Swanhild raised an eyebrow. 'Are you sure?'

'Yes,' said Rutger. 'I know I want to learn magic. And when you know you have to do something painful, it is best not to think too hard about it. My father told me that. So do it — now, before I change my mind.'

'As you wish.' Swanhild took the stone out of her pouch again, and stood up. 'Come here.'

Rutger stood, too. He could feel himself sweating worse than ever, but he didn't hesitate. He took off his coat and hung it from a tree, then untied the front of his shirt. He pulled it open, exposing his chest. 'What do I need to do?'

Swanhild looked around, and then pointed. 'Stand with your back to that tree — you will need something to support you.'

He went to the tree and stood against it, gripping a branch. 'It might knock me over, then?'

'Yes, it might,' said Swanhild. 'You should clean yourself as well; you don't want any dirt inside you.'

Rutger grimaced. He picked up a handful of fresh snow and rubbed it over his chest, cleaning away the layer of dirt that had covered it since his last bath. The cold numbed his skin, and he was glad about that.

Swanhild stood just in front of him, holding the sapphire. She reached out and touched his chest, feeling the skin and the bone underneath. The feel of her fingers on his skin made him shiver — she was so warm, and it thrilled him to have her this close to him, even at such a moment.

Swanhild found the spot she must have been looking for, and pressed the stone against his skin, just over his breastbone.

'Will you—?' Rutger started to ask, but his words were cut off. A jolt went through him as the stone shot straight through his skin. He felt a crunch deep inside his chest, and screamed more out of shock than pain, which came an instant later. But, worse: he felt the stone. It was there, inside him, burning like a hot coal, and as he looked down at himself he saw it. Swanhild's hand was still there, over the wound on his chest, and blue light had begun to glow around the hole the stone had left. It was the same blue as the sapphire. He saw it shining through the blood that trickled down over his stomach and soaked into his shirt. It made little veins in his exposed flesh, and shone on Swanhild's pale fingers as she pulled her hand away. Rutger saw the ugly hole in his body, edged with ragged skin. And there, past the thin layer of muscle, he could see his own exposed bone. He started to retch.

But even as he reached up to try to cover the wound, it started to heal over. The blue light intensified, and the hole in his breastbone sealed over. Muscle grew on top of that, and then skin, marked by a deep scar. The pain stopped at once.

Rutger heard his own harsh breathing as he sagged against the tree. His fingers found the scar, and he rubbed it compulsively. He could feel the stone inside, throbbing gently in time to his heartbeat. It was done.

'There,' said Swanhild, reaching over to touch his shoulder. 'It's over. Well done.'

Rutger couldn't stop touching the scar. 'It's in me …'

'Yes, that's right,' said Swanhild. 'It will stay a part of you until you die. But don't expect it to heal you every time you are injured; it only does that the first time.'

'Shame,' Rutger managed.

'Yes, it is a shame,' Swanhild agreed. 'Come, sit down by the fire and I will get you something to eat. You should be fine now.'

Rutger let her lead him to the fire, and sat down on his log. He could feel himself shaking with shock. But there was more to it than that. A strange warmth had begun to fill his veins and muscles; a vitality that had never been there before. He felt exhausted and energised at the same time, and a ferocious excitement gripped him — a sense that he could do anything, as if nothing was beyond his reach now.

'You can feel it, can't you?' said Swanhild, apparently guessing what he was thinking. 'The magic.'

Rutger had started to grin. 'Yes,' he said, taking the bread she was offering him. He bit into it, and, even though it was dry and rough, it tasted more delicious than anything he could ever remember having tasted before. Everything had started to feel more intense; sight, sound, taste and smell. He wanted to laugh.

Swanhild watched him with a hint of amusement. 'It'll wear off, so enjoy it while it lasts,' she said.

Rutger only half-heard her. He ate ravenously while he looked around the clearing, taking it all in as if for the first time. Everything was highlighted by bright blue and golden sparks, which danced through the air like fairies. The smell of pine needles and snow made him feel clean inside and out. And Swanhild … She looked even more beautiful than before. He was in such a wild mood just then that he almost said so.

She, meanwhile, was sitting opposite with a satisfied expression. 'Today I realised a dream which has taken me years,' she said. 'I have given the gift of magic to a free man.'

Rutger studied his hands, half expecting them to be glowing. But they looked like their normal grubby, callused selves. Now he was starting to come back down to earth; the lights in the air were fading, and the powerful scents with them. He tried to cling to them, never wanting them to go, but they slipped out of his grasp and left him feeling tired and slightly disappointed. He looked up at Swanhild. 'Thank you. I'll never forget this.'

'It would be hard to forget!' she smiled. 'Congratulations, Rutger von Gothendorf. From this day onward, you'll never be an ordinary furrier again. And now I can start teaching you how to use your new gift — immediately, if you feel ready for it.'

'Yes!' Rutger stood bolt upright. 'Teach me now: I want to use it!'

'Then we'll begin,' said Swanhild. 'Come with me.'

*

Swanhild led him up onto the hill behind the clearing — the same direction he had gone in his dream. He was too excited to care much when he saw that there was nothing but perfectly ordinary forest on the other side.

On the hilltop, Swanhild had made an ordinary fireplace; just wood neatly stacked inside a ring of stones. She pointed to it. 'See if you can light it.'

'But—' Rutger began uncertainly.

'Don't think too hard!' Swanhild interrupted. 'Just point at the wood and think of fire.'

Rutger pointed his palm at the heap of wood, the way he had seen her do it, and pictured it bursting into flame. Nothing happened. But he remembered what Swanhild had said about channelling energy, so he started to focus on that as well. He let himself feel the power pulsating in his chest. Yes, it was there, and when he concentrated on it he felt it respond. It rose up inside him, as if he were about to vomit it out, but he pushed back. It felt bizarre — a new part of himself, something he could flex like a muscle. The stone pulsated harder, spreading energy through his body. It almost felt as though it were fighting back against him, overwhelming his system like a drug. He started to panic.

'It's all right,' Swanhild said from somewhere far away. 'You don't have to—'

Rutger ignored her. He fought back against the fear, even as it threatened to overtake him. *No*, he thought. *No, you're mine. I control you.* The magic rushed through him even more powerfully, burning inside every fibre of his body. *I control you*, he told it. *I control you!* He thought it over and over, pushing back at the rampaging energy, and little by little it calmed down. It belonged to him. It was a part of him.

The magic began to surge again, but he angrily shoved it back and channelled it into his arm and down into his palm. *Fire*, he thought, and bright blue flames shot from his hand and onto the heap of wood, which instantly caught alight. His flames kept coming, though, pouring out of him and onto the ground, completely enveloping the fireplace.

'Stop!' Swanhild yelled. 'Stop now!'

With a supreme effort, Rutger pulled the magic back. The flames stopped coming, and he staggered backward against a tree. He was trembling, and the sapphire inside him burned.

At his feet, the fireplace had completely disintegrated into a heap of bluish coals and blackened stones.

Even Swanhild looked slightly shocked. 'Well done.'

Rutger coughed, and winced when it made his chest hurt. 'I didn't mean to do that ... There was just so much of it.'

'No, it's fine,' said Swanhild. 'Come here.' She took him by the arm and gently helped him back down the hill toward her hut.

'I'm sorry,' said Rutger. 'I made a mistake.'

Swanhild laughed as she helped him sit down on his log. 'Don't apologise! What you just did, I've never seen anyone do that before. I honestly didn't think you'd be able to do anything on your first try; I only meant for you to start learning how to feel the magic inside you.'

Rutger looked up blearily. 'Really?'

'Yes,' said Swanhild. 'Your control is astonishing. You must be very talented.'

Rutger coughed again. 'I don't feel talented. Right now I feel exhausted.'

'Well, you would be,' said Swanhild. 'But that's enough for today. We can work again tomorrow. For now you should go home and get some rest.'

He nodded. 'Yes, you're right. I won't be able to get anything done in the workshop today. I'm not sure I even have the energy to check my traps.'

'Never mind; you rest here and I'll do it for you,' said Swanhild. 'And,' she paused. 'I don't have to tell you not to try any more magic without me there, do I?'

'No, you don't.'

'Good,' said Swanhild. 'I'll be back soon.'

Chapter 7

After that, Rutger went to the clearing every day to see Swanhild and continue their lessons together. He still carried his sword with him, but only for appearances; now his mornings were spent practising the basic spells Swanhild taught him. As he soon learned, it was easy enough to destroy things; all that took was wild bursts of raw energy. The more delicate things were much harder. He could lift an object with magic, but making small motions with it was much more difficult than simply hurling it. And he could blast something into ashes with fire, but making a small enough flame to light a cooking fire took a lot of concentration and care.

'You see now why I had to be so careful,' Swanhild told him early on. 'This kind of power in the wrong hands — it wouldn't even take a bad person. Plain carelessness would be enough. But you obviously have the sense to know better than that!'

Rutger nodded bashfully. 'It's hard, but if I can't control it properly I'll never do anything useful with it.'

He was eager to get to that point, so he arrived quickly every morning and worked his hardest, leaving Swanhild to check the mink traps while he rested. She was quite good at it, and came back with more mink than she really should have been expected to, although Rutger almost immediately guessed why.

'You can use magic to hunt?' he asked.

'Yes, of course,' said Swanhild, offering up a bundle of freshly killed white mink. 'I dragged them out of their burrows.'

'I think I should learn how to do that,' said Rutger. 'It would definitely help my business. And maybe I could skin them with magic as well.'

Swanhild smiled and shrugged. 'Yes, why not? It would be a useful challenge as well. I'm certain the Jüngen would call it blasphemous, using magic for practical things, but who cares what they think?'

Rutger laughed. 'Exactly!'

He ended up staying so long that day that they had lunch together before he left. It wasn't the first time this had happened, so Rutger had brought some food which he shared with Swanhild over the blue fire he had lit.

'You know,' he said thoughtfully, 'Swanhild, I think you might be the best friend I ever had.'

'That's kind of you to say,' she said.

'I mean it!' said Rutger. 'Before you came, I was the village oddball. Everyone laughed at me behind my back, said I'd gone strange in the head since Horst died. My brothers were my only real friends, and they thought I was odd as well. But you're not like them. You treat me as if I am ordinary.'

Swanhild's strange red eyes shone in the firelight. 'But you are not ordinary, are you?' she said. 'You are very extraordinary, Rutger.'

'I'm only different because I have magic,' he said shyly. 'And you gave that to me.'

'But your talent is what sets you apart,' said Swanhild. She indicated the fire between them. 'That fire there — most magic users would take months to learn how to make one of those. Some never manage to do it at all. But you mastered it in weeks. In all my years I have never met anyone who could do that. But it makes me proud to know that my instinct about you was right.'

'Oh, well ... thank you,' said Rutger, pleasantly embarrassed.

'I mean it,' said Swanhild. 'But now I think the time has come for us to decide what to do next. You are learning fast, and you will need to decide what to do with your skills. Unless you plan to stay here and use them to catch mink?'

Rutger shook his head. 'I don't want to leave, but maybe I will have to. Everyone *expects* me to. But where would I go? To join the rebels? To fight in Drucht Valley?'

'This is something you need to think hard about,' said Swanhild. 'You need to remember who you are, Rutger. You are the only commoner to have learned magic. You are not corrupted by Jüngen teachings. Your loyalty is yours to give to whoever or whatever you choose. The rebels might welcome you, but they might well not: you could pretend to be a former Jünger, but they would see through it soon enough. The ordinary people would be suspicious of you, too. But you could still help either one if you choose. But you can't fight the Jüngen alone.'

'But I could try,' Rutger muttered. 'Anyway, what about you?' he said aloud. 'What will *you* do? You're alone as well, aren't you?'

'Oh, I'll go with you,' said Swanhild. 'I still have more to teach you. And as you say, I'm alone as well.'

A hot, forbidden excitement raced up Rutger's spine. 'If I leave, I leave with you,' he decided. 'And I'll be happy to go. I just wish you could have met my family.'

Swanhild looked thoughtful. 'Actually, I think I could,' she said. 'I have an idea.'

'What is it?' asked Rutger. 'You'll come into the village?'

'It wouldn't be right to leave without saying goodbye,' said Swanhild. 'Your family would worry. Why don't we visit them together, and you can introduce me? We can say I'm from a neighbouring village, and that we met accidentally in the forest. You can tell the truth and say that you have been coming here to meet me. And now you're ready to give your family the good news: you and I are going to move away together and get married.'

Rutger wanted to laugh with disbelief, but he didn't. He cast a longing look at Swanhild and said; 'Yes, that could work. That way, so far as everyone is concerned, I moved away to start a new life. If anyone comes looking for us later, they won't hear anything suspicious. And that way you get to meet my family as well. They'll like you; I'm sure of it.'

'Agreed, then,' said Swanhild.

'When should we go?' asked Rutger. 'I need to take some time first: I'll leave my business to Gerhart, and Rocco can support him until he is ready to work alone. But I'll sell some of my things, so we have some money to take with us. And we should buy a pair of deer for the journey, if we can afford it.'

'There is no great hurry,' said Swanhild. 'Take the time you need, and tell me when you are ready. And first you need to decide where we should go.'

'Well, where do *you* think we should go?' Rutger asked.

'It depends,' said Swanhild. 'Who do you want to fight for? The rebels or the common people?'

'The common people,' said Rutger. 'I don't owe the rebels anything. But the commoners won't accept my magic, as you said.'

'Well then, I think the best thing to do would be to prove ourselves to them,' said Swanhild. 'Do something to show them we want to help.'

Rutger nodded. 'But what? Do you know?'

'There is a Jünger in the upper part of Drucht Valley,' said Swanhild. 'He rules a city called Drachenburg, and his name is Warin. Have you heard of him?'

'I don't think so,' said Rutger. 'Who is he?'

'One of the most powerful Jüngen in the country,' said Swanhild. 'He climbed the Jünger hierarchy by murdering at least ten people. The destruction in Drucht Valley is all his doing, in the Drachengott's name.' She paused, and her mouth tightened. 'It was Warin who ordered the destruction of my home. Out of all the Jüngen, he is probably the most hated. If we can kill him, it would send a powerful message — to the Jüngen, and the rebels, and to the Drachengott himself.'

'Warin,' Rutger repeated.

'You may know him already,' said Swanhild. 'About ten years ago he was near Gothendorf with his brother Reinhard, on a mission to scout the forests here.'

Rutger's stomach lurched. 'Wait, you don't mean—?'

'Yes, it may well have been them you saw here in this clearing,' said Swanhild. 'If my guess is correct, it was Warin and Reinhard who killed your brother. And if not ... well, they still deserve to die.'

'I'll do it,' Rutger said grimly. 'Let's both do it. For your family, and mine.'

Chapter 8

A few days later, Rutger's family gathered together in the home of his eldest surviving brother, Kurt. Kurt, who worked as a carpenter with the help of his wife and three sons, owned the biggest house and had offered to host everyone, which was just as well. All of Rutger's siblings were there, and along with Kurt's family there was also his sister Petra with her own family, his second elder brother Arnwald with his wife and six children, not to mention three aunts, an uncle, and Horst's widow Odila with her two daughters. Rutger, Rocco and Gerhart barely managed to find room at the table, although Rutger had been given Kurt's usual seat at the head. He took it gratefully and helped himself to some food. Normally he couldn't stand big family gatherings like this one — the noise alone was enough to drive anyone mad, not to mention the bickering. But tonight was different. Tonight, Swanhild was sitting beside him.

He had thrilled at the experience of walking through the village with her. Crazy Rutger, strolling back out of the forest with a beautiful woman at his side. The guards up on the gate had stared in frank amazement, and he had nodded back as if this was nothing out of the ordinary. In the village itself everyone else had stared too, and plenty had come over to ask who in the world this stranger was.

Swanhild had surprised him. She had always seemed so confident to him, but here in the village she looked a little uneasy; even nervous. Even now she still looked nervy, even as various children came over to say hello to her and shyly ask her where she had come from.

'I came here from Odorf,' she said shortly, keeping close to Rutger's side. 'It's a village on the other side of the forest.'

Rutger patted her hand to reassure her; not something he would normally have done, but if she was going to pose as his betrothed he should help her act the part. Besides, he wanted to do it. Her skin felt as wonderfully warm as always.

Kurt leaned over to talk to them from his seat on Rutger's other side. 'Are you all right, Helga?' he asked, using the false name Swanhild had given.

She smiled awkwardly. 'Forgive me — it's been a long time since I was around so many people.'

Kurt grinned back. 'Don't worry, they're harmless. More or less. But isn't it time you introduced yourself properly to everyone?'

Swanhild turned to Rutger. 'You should speak to them, Rutchen,' she said.

Rutger laughed. 'Nobody ever called me Rutchen except for my mother.'

'Well, it suits you,' said Swanhild.

'She's right; it does,' said Kurt.

Beside him, his wife said; 'You're blushing, Rutchen!'

Rutger glanced at Swanhild as the others joined in the laughter. She nodded back, and the two of them stood up. Silence fell, and everyone looked expectantly at the pair of them.

'I think you know why you are all here,' said Rutger, taking Swanhild's hand as he spoke. 'This is Helga, from Odorf. She and I met in the forest — we came into it from opposite sides, and stumbled across each other by chance. Every day since then we have been meeting there in secret. I hope none of you are upset with me for keeping her a secret; the truth is I have been begging her to let me bring her back here to meet you.'

'It's true; it's my fault,' said Swanhild. She looked bashful. 'The truth is ... I was afraid you wouldn't like me.'

'Oh, don't say that!' said Odile, while the others shook their heads and groaned in playful disbelief. 'I don't see anything wrong with her,' she added. 'Do you?'

'Not me!' said Kurt. 'She looks lovely and kind.'

Rutger glanced happily at Swanhild. 'You see — I told you they would like you. As you can see, I persuaded her.'

'Well, it's wonderful to meet you,' said Rocco. 'We all hoped Rutger would find someone to love.'

The others nodded and murmured congratulations. Rutger kept his eyes on Swanhild, and a fierce longing squeezed him by the heart. He almost felt giddy, and a mad impulse came over him to lean over and kiss her. But he couldn't bring himself to do it, even if the others were expecting it. He couldn't take advantage of her, even if this had been her idea.

He coughed, and swallowed his queasiness. 'Anyway,' he said, trying his best to sound normal and happy, 'I think you know what we are here to announce.' He gave Swanhild's hand a squeeze. 'Helga and I are going to marry. We have decided to move away to the coast and begin a new life together.'

'You're going away?' said Gerhart.

'Yes,' Rutger said sadly. 'I think you all knew I would one day. There are too many memories for me here. I can't keep living in a dream. I've made myself into the village laughing-stock. But with my Helga, I can leave all that behind and try to have a normal life. She has shown me the way to be happy again.'

'That's beautiful, Rutger,' said Petra. 'I'm so glad to hear it. And you're right: everyone did expect you to leave. But not like this. We thought you would take your sword and run away to fight in the valley, and none of us truly wanted that. This leaving is much better. It's right for you, and we will be happier to know it than to believe you were putting yourself in danger for the sake of some mad dream.'

Guilt chewed at Rutger's stomach, but he kept his smile in place. 'Thank you, Petra. That's well said, and you are right. Helga and I plan to leave soon — once I have sold some of my things and we are ready for the journey. Gerhart, I'm leaving my workshop to you, and Rocco can help you keep it. You know everything you need to know to make a living now.'

'Thank you!' said Gerhart. 'I'll take good care of it.'

'I know you will,' said Rutger. 'And Rocco, I can trust you to help him, can't I?'

'Of course you can,' said Rocco, reaching over to ruffle his younger brother's hair. 'I can keep this one out of trouble. And you will send word to us once you have found your new home, won't you, Rutger?'

'The instant,' said Rutger.

'We'll come and join you for the wedding, then,' said Petra. 'As many of us who can come. But I think we can all do our part here in Gothendorf, yes?' She looked around at the others

'Yes, of course,' said Arnwald. 'You might not be married yet, but you can have your wedding gifts from us before you leave. And tonight — well, tonight we can celebrate!'

Everyone cheered.

'Thank you,' said Rutger. 'Thank you all of you.'

'Thank you so much,' said Swanhild. 'You're a fine family; I can see why my Rutchen is so sweet, if this is where he came from.'

It was a good way to end the announcement, and after that the important discussions ended as the betrothal party began. Everyone had brought some food and something to drink, and they sat together and talked, ate, drank and sang songs long into the night. There was smoked sausage and good cheese, fresh bread brought by Rocco, who had also brought along a batch of his best pear and blackberry pies. And Petra, whose husband was a brewer, had brought plenty of beer. Everyone came over to talk to Rutger and Swanhild privately, offering their congratulations and good wishes, and promising to provide them with a gift for their journey. Swanhild accepted gracefully, seeming more relaxed now, but Rutger had to struggle to make himself relax and enjoy the evening. The sight of everyone so happy just made him feel dirty. And what would they all do when he never did send word? They would worry that he had lost all his money, or even been killed. And if he *was* killed — if he went to Drachenburg and died there — what would they think of him then? They would all know him for a liar and a fool, who had done exactly what they had all feared he would.

Rutger couldn't stop thinking about that, and it completely ruined the night for him. And what made it even worse was Swanhild, sitting there looking so relaxed, so close that their hands and arms kept brushing against each other when they reached for their mugs. A thousand things went through his head when he looked at her; a million words he wanted to say to her but couldn't seem to actually speak, each one even wilder and more stupid than the last. And besides, what was the use? She was his teacher, and she was beautiful and wise. She knew a hundred things he didn't. And even if she wasn't a noblewoman, she still carried herself like one. She would never want anything to do with an ignorant furrier like him, even if he did have magic now. But having her there, now, pretending to be in love with him, was an agony just as bad as his guilt.

For the rest of the evening, Rutger said very little and let Swanhild carry things along. He half expected someone to ask him why he was looking so miserable, but nobody did — perhaps his mask of happiness hadn't slipped after all. But he had a feeling that it would only get harder to hold onto for the next few days.

*

Swanhild stayed with Kurt that night, since there wasn't enough room for her in Rutger's house — and besides that, it wasn't proper for a couple to live together until they were married. The next day she came to meet Rutger at his workshop, and the two of them got to work gathering up some of his belongings to sell.

Before they left, however, Rutger opened a box in the corner of the workshop and brought out a bundle of cloth. 'Here,' he said, offering it to her. 'I made this for you.'

Swanhild unwrapped the package. Inside was a fine coat lined with mink fur, its hem decorated with a row of black-tipped white tails. She touched it, rolling a tail between her fingers, her expression unreadable.

'Do you like it?' Rutger asked nervously. 'I thought it would keep you warm on our journey.'

Swanhild finally smiled. 'It's beautiful — thank you.'

Rutger smiled back, mostly with relief. 'Try it on — I hope it fits.'

She pulled it over her shoulders. It fitted perfectly, and she reached up and pulled the hood up over her head. 'It feels wonderful,' she said. 'So soft.'

'The outside is good deer leather, so it should protect you from the wind and the rain,' said Rutger. 'But I wanted it to look beautiful as well. But you could make an old rag look beautiful.' He blurted out the last part before he could stop himself, and Gerhart, who was helping them, smirked to himself.

Swanhild didn't laugh, though. 'Thank you,' she said. 'That's so sweet of you. I'll treasure it.'

'Thank you,' Rutger echoed. Words had failed him again. But while they worked to gather the rest of his things and then take them to the people he hoped would buy them, he couldn't stop himself from watching her and proudly observing how his gift fitted so flatteringly around her slim body and the way the mink tails swung when she moved.

They were able to sell off most of Rutger's unwanted possessions for a few thaler, and they traded an old wooden clothes chest of his for a couple of tough canvas packs. Swanhild had brought over a few things from her hut in the forest; mostly spare clothes. Of course, with magic at her command, she wouldn't need to carry much. Magic could replace just about any tool, as he had learned.

Rutger and Swanhild packed their bags, adding some food for the first part of the journey. But that afternoon, just as they were about to go and enquire about the price of a good pair of deer, one of Kurt's sons arrived at the door looking breathless and eager. 'Come with me — we have something special to show you!'

'We had better do as he says,' Swanhild said playfully. 'If it's special.'

'It is,' said the boy. 'Hurry up!'

He dashed off, and Rutger and Swanhild followed him. He ran straight back to Kurt's house, and there everyone was waiting for them — all gathered around a pair of fine stags. Kurt and Arnwald were holding the reins, and the two animals shifted restlessly and huffed.

Rutger stopped at the sight of them. 'You didn't!' he exclaimed.

'We did!' said Kurt. He came over, leading his deer. 'Two good deer, just for you and with all our love. You can thank Aunt Linza for the saddles.'

Rutger reached up to pat the deer's muzzle. It was a big, healthy-looking animal, still wearing a touch of its winter coat, although by now spring was well advanced. A small, light saddle had been strapped to the animal's back, and a pair of saddlebags on its haunches. Its antlers had been decorated with bells.

'Look in the saddlebags,' Arnwald added, while Swanhild petted her own deer. 'You can thank *me* for what's inside.'

Rutger opened the nearest one. It had been packed tightly with food: bread and travel cakes, and even a small wheel of cheese. He turned and hugged Arnwald fiercely. 'Thank you! Thank you so much — all of you!' He hugged Kurt as well, and leathery Aunt Linza, and everyone else, his heart swelling.

They patted him on the back or kissed him on the cheeks, all very good-natured.

'You just make us proud!' said Petra. 'Take care of yourself and Helga, and send word as soon as you find your new home!'

'But come back here and visit!' said Odila. 'As soon as you have your first child — that would be a good time!'

In the end it was almost impossible to leave. They spent that night at Kurt's house again, for a second celebratory meal, intending to leave at dawn the next day. As it was, the farewells went on for so long that it wasn't until almost noon that Rutger and Swanhild finally climbed onto their deer and began the ride out of the village. The family all followed, calling out last good wishes, until finally the couple passed through the gates and went on alone, although Rutger kept twisting around in the saddle to wave.

When they had crossed the field and entered the forest, the silence felt very sudden. Rutger hadn't had much experience in deerback riding, but his steed was docile enough. The beast walked in among the trees, soft-footed and calm, with Swanhild's own deer taking up the rear. Only stags were used for riding by adults, since they were bigger and more robust. These two looked good and sturdy to Rutger, and he silently thanked his family once again for them.

'They gave us a good gift,' said Swanhild, apparently thinking the same thing. 'These deer will take us a long way.'

'Yes,' Rutger muttered. 'Of course they don't know how far we really plan to go.'

'Don't torment yourself,' said Swanhild. 'I know how bad you feel for lying to them, but you must know that it was necessary.'

'Of course I do,' said Rutger. 'But that doesn't make me feel any better. I lied to all of them, and took these deer dishonestly. Wedding gifts for a wedding that won't ever happen!'

'But your family will be safe now,' said Swanhild. 'And trust me: Jüngen will want to find them if you and I succeed. But from now on, neither of us has ever been to Gothendorf, and the Rutger who lived there has gone to the coast. But if that doesn't comfort you, then think of this: what we plan to do isn't for our benefit, but theirs. Theirs and every other ordinary person in Wendland. Because, unless Warin is killed, his armies will come down through the valley and destroy Gothendorf and every other free settlement. One day, your family will understand.'

'I suppose you're right,' said Rutger and, even though he sounded reluctant, he did feel better hearing her put it this way. 'What we did was necessary. And once this is all over I can go back there and apologise to them.'

'Yes, you can,' said Swanhild. 'For now, they're safe. And soon there will be no traces left for anyone to follow.'

Rutger's deer walked on up the slope through the forest, and finally entered the clearing where Swanhild's hut stood. There, Rutger reined in the animal and dismounted. The deer made a *grarg* sound in its throat while Rutger tied its reins to a low-hanging branch. Behind him, Swanhild tied up her own mount, and the two of them went over to the hut on foot.

Rutger glanced back at the deer. 'Won't this scare them?'

'It will, but they should get used to it,' said Swanhild. 'We don't want them to panic later, in a more dangerous situation.'

Rutger shrugged and pointed his palms toward the hut. Swanhild did the same, and in the instant before they began Rutger felt that thrill which came to him every time he used magic. He concentrated, and let the energy come flowing out of his chest and down his arms. The sapphire throbbed inside him, and blue fire rushed out of his skin and into the hut, mingling with Swanhild's silver. The hut burned so quickly and fiercely under their onslaught that it crumbled to ashes in a matter of moments. A couple of trees behind it caught alight, but Rutger pulled water out of the ground and doused the flames.

'Good work,' said Swanhild. She walked over onto the patch of blackened ground where her hut had been, while Rutger went to check on the deer. They were shifting nervously, but not outright panicking, and they relaxed again as he murmured and patted them. He turned to see what Swanhild was doing. She was standing in the middle of the hut's ashes, and now waved at him to join her.

He came over, eyeing the burnt ground and the trees. 'Well, the hut's gone,' he said, 'but I don't know how we'll hide this.'

'We can do it,' said Swanhild. 'It's time to learn a new spell. Come and take my hand.'

Rutger went to her side and took her hand. 'Those two Jüngen held hands,' he recalled. 'Can we share magic or something?'

'Very good,' said Swanhild. 'That's it exactly. We can join our magic, and cast more powerful spells that way. Now, let your magic come down your arm to our hands.'

Practice had made it much easier for Rutger to control the energy which thrummed through his body every moment. He let it flow down his arm as instructed, just as he had done a hundred times before, but this time it was different. He felt Swanhild's hand grow even warmer in his, as her own magic came down to meet his, and the moment the two powers met their linked hands began to glow with a silvery-blue light. Rutger gasped at the sight of it. 'It's so beautiful! And look: it's a mix of both our colours!'

'I knew they would look good together,' said Swanhild. 'But now, let's use it. Let my magic guide yours.'

Rutger felt her magic move downward, and sent his after it. A thin beam of silver-blue left their hands and went into the ground, soaking into the earth like water.

A moment later, the ashy floor of the clearing began to bristle with green. New shoots thrust their way out of the soil, twisting to face the sun. Flowers popped open before his eyes, and small shrubs sprouted. Even a couple of saplings grew, their trunks thickening as their branches reached for the forest canopy. Rutger watched it all in astonishment, too awestruck to move, and not wanting to either.

Finally, Swanhild let go of his hand. He felt a curious sense of loss as they parted, and not just because they were no longer physically touching. He stopped his magic, and lost the extra warmth it had given him when it was mixed with Swanhild's. The sapphire burned gently in his chest.

'There,' Swanhild said softly. 'Look at our clearing now.'

Rutger turned slowly, taking it all in. Once the clearing had been barren, even before the hut's destruction. But now it was thick with new life; lush with grass and sweetened by flowers. A small honey-eating bird flitted out from the trees and began to dart between them, stopping to perch in a shaft of golden sunlight which sparkled with pollen.

'It's perfect,' said Rutger, smiling in wonder.

'No one will ever find anything here now,' said Swanhild. 'They would have to dig to find those ashes, and if they found those or noticed the blackening on the tree trunks, what would that prove? Only that there was a fire here a long time ago.'

'I'm glad we could leave it like this,' said Rutger. 'We never recovered Horst's body, you know. But now this can be his resting place. And it's the place where we first met as well,' he added. 'I'll never forget it.'

'And now we can remember it like this,' said Swanhild, gesturing at the beauty around them.

'Yes.' Rutger turned back toward her, and for a moment their eyes met. She looked so perfect standing there among the flowers, the sunlight catching her hair and almost making it glow. Her rich red-brown eyes were alight, shining, fixed on his. That longing rose in him again; that aching need to touch her, to hold her, to kiss her.

He didn't move.

Finally, Swanhild looked away. 'We should go,' she said awkwardly. 'We have a long way to travel.'

Something died inside Rutger, as it did every time a moment like this had come and he had let it pass by. 'Yes,' he said. 'We should get out of the forest, too. I don't want to be attacked by spiders or worse.'

'Yes ... or worse,' Swanhild said grimly.

Chapter 9

Rather than retrace their steps, they stuck to what they had told Rutger's family they had been going to do, and went on through the forest toward the other side, where the village of Odorf lay. Rutger had never visited it, and people from Gothendorf rarely went there since it meant passing through the forest, which not many people were eager to do. Rutger and Swanhild got through it uneventfully enough, though, which was almost a disappointment to Rutger. If he encountered a giant spider now, he would take some satisfaction from being able to deal with the creature. They wouldn't be much of a danger to him now. One quick blast of flame and he would send them scurrying.

'I have an idea,' he said after a while. 'Why don't we practise with our magic while we ride along? So the deer can get used to it? If we're attacked, it would be better if we could fight on deerback.'

'You could be right,' Swanhild said thoughtfully. 'But we need to be careful — let me try it first.'

They were riding side by side now, and Rutger watched as Swanhild shot a quick bolt of flame from her palm at a nearby tree trunk. Her deer started, but she pulled the animal back under control without much trouble.

'There, that wasn't too bad,' said Rutger. 'Let me try it now.' He threw a small blue fireball between his deer's antlers and it hit the ground in front of them. The deer reared up, almost throwing him off. He wrestled with the reins, shouting, 'Woah! Woah, there — it's all right!'

The deer bucked around in a circle, but Rutger managed to get it to settle down before he lost his seat. Swanhild's deer retreated, huffing in agitation, and once things had calmed down Swanhild laughed at him. 'Idiot.'

Rutger sagged over his deer's neck, panting. 'All right, that was stupid.'

'Yes, it was,' said Swanhild. 'Maybe next time you should do something smaller.'

'Yes, I think so,' said Rutger. 'But let's rest for the time being.'

After that they were both more cautious, but Rutger stuck to his plan. Every now and then he would let off a quick blast of magic; this time to the side or up into the air. Swanhild did the same, and bit by bit the deer became accustomed to it. By the time they reached the far side of the forest that evening, the deer had stopped shying altogether. Of course Rutger didn't fool himself by thinking that would make them stay calm if it ever came to a real fight. But it was a start.

They began to see signs of civilisation again toward the forest's edge. As they came down from the hills the trees grew thinner, and in the lowlands some of them had been cut down. More and more stumps appeared along the way, until they finally came across a couple of people busy loading fresh wood onto a cart. The sun had begun to go down, and the woodcutters weren't much more than silhouettes against the darkening sky.

Swanhild held up the lamp she had lit, and called out. 'Hello!'

The woodcutters stopped work and turned to look at them. In the lamplight they turned out to be not men, as Rutger had expected, but a couple of burly women.

'Hello,' said one of them. 'People coming out of the forest? You're not elves, are you?'

Swanhild laughed. 'No, just travellers. Tell us, are you from Odorf?'

'Yes, we are,' said the second woman. 'Where did you two come from?'

'Bonndorf,' Swanhild lied. 'We're on our way to the coast, and we were hoping to stay in Odorf for the night.'

'You're in luck, then,' said the woodcutter. 'There's a tavern in Odorf with rooms to spare. They even have half-decent beer. But where are you going?'

'Burgund,' said Rutger. 'Near the Gallien border. We plan to start a new life there.'

'I hope you speak Gallisch, then,' said the second woodcutter. 'Half the people in Burgund speak nothing else, from what I've heard. Anyway, Odorf is that way. Not far.'

Rutger and Swanhild thanked the two women, and joined the road just beyond the forest's edge. A few lamps sat on posts to light their way, and ahead they could see the lights of the village itself. The deer trotted wearily on toward it, and Rutger privately gave thanks for the sake of his backside. He'd heard the term 'saddle sores' before, but now he was starting to learn just what that actually meant, and he didn't like it one bit.

As for Odorf itself, it was something of a disappointment for the first place he had seen outside his birthplace. Of course it wasn't that far away from Gothendorf, but it still looked more similar to it than he had expected. Like Gothendorf, it had a wall around it, and the houses on the other side were tiled and had white walls with black beams. But unlike Gothendorf Odorf sat beside a river, which flowed past its walls on the opposite side to the gates where Rutger and Swanhild entered.

'The River Vent,' said Swanhild. 'It will take us where we need to go. Up through the mountains and into Drucht Valley.'

'How long do you think it will take us?' asked Rutger.

'I'm not sure,' said Swanhild. 'Three or four weeks, maybe. It depends on the ground, and whether anyone troubles us along the way. But once we go into the mountains we can practise our magic again; nobody will see us there.'

'Unless there are dragons,' said Rutger. 'Would they be in the mountains?'

'Yes, they could be,' said Swanhild. She paused. 'I think we should start to plan how to fight them. A fight with a dragon is serious.'

'I hardly know anything about them,' said Rutger.

'Then I will teach you,' said Swanhild.

*

They stayed in Odorf that night, and set out again in the morning as agreed. The road which had brought them into the village followed the River Vent north-east toward the distant mountains, and they followed it through the farmlands which took up most of this part of the county. It was beautiful along the river, and Rutger enjoyed it, even if riding all day was tiring and often dull. So many new sights helped to keep things interesting. Willows, birches and poplar trees grew on the river banks, and the fields on both sides were thick with new growth; wheat and barley, corn, melons and potatoes. Other fields had been set aside for livestock; they saw cows, sheep and goats, and once a herd of deer. Geese wandered along the road or swam in the river, and once or twice the travellers came across orchards of apples, pears and peaches.

It was so quiet here that Rutger found it hard to believe that there could be so much trouble happening on the other side of the mountains. The people were just as peaceful as the land they lived in; most of them more than happy to pass the time of day and sell some produce, or invite the travellers to stay for the night in exchange for some stories about the places they had been.

'Good people, living in a good land,' Swanhild agreed when Rutger told her how much he liked it here. 'And most of them can have no idea of what could happen to them.'

'How could it?' said Rutger. 'Why does the Drachengott hate us so much? I mean, I know we rebelled against him, but we're not doing any harm. Why can't he just leave us alone?'

'I don't know,' said Swanhild. 'I don't think anyone truly knows. The Jüngen believe it's because Gottlosen like us deserve to be punished, and that our lands should be in their hands because all lands belong to the Drachengott. He made them, after all — or so some people believe.'

'Do *you* believe it?' asked Rutger.

'I'm not sure,' she answered. 'And maybe it doesn't matter so much. What matters is that we have an enemy and, even if we do defeat his minions, we would one day have to defeat him as well.'

'But how?' said Rutger. 'I mean, he's a god.'

'But there could be a way,' said Swanhild. 'Yes, there could be a way, if we can find it. If the Jüngen were destroyed, it would make a great difference. The Drachengott never leaves his mountain. He can't.'

'But the other dragons can,' Rutger said grimly.

'Yes, and you're right,' said Swanhild, 'they might well be in the mountains. But at least you know they aren't invincible. You have that sword as proof.'

Rutger fingered the dragon-horn handle. He had decided to keep the sword, if only for its sentimental value. Besides, it was a great boasting-point to have a sword with a handle made from dragon horn.

'Can we fight dragons with magic?' he asked now.

'Yes, we can,' said Swanhild. 'Dragons themselves have no magic other than the fire they breathe. They are never given stones.'

'Then how do they channel the energy they need to breathe fire?' said Rutger.

Swanhild smiled. 'Clever question. They take it directly from their maker: the Drachengott. All dragons are part of him; pieces of his soul given independent lives. His most high-ranking Jüngen are given the ability to summon dragons — to use a piece of the Drachengott's power to create a new dragon at will. That dragon will serve the Jünger who summoned it until death. But others are independent; created by the Drachengott directly and obedient only to him. I think he keeps them separate in case his Jüngen ever turn on him and need to be destroyed. But the dragons themselves can never be a danger to the Drachengott. As part of him, they have no power to harm him or even disobey him.'

'They sound like slaves,' said Rutger, fascinated. He had never heard any of this before.

'They are,' said Swanhild, her mouth tightening. 'Slaves to the Drachengott, or to his Jüngen. And none of them even know it.'

'So we'll have to fight them,' said Rutger. 'What's the best way? Fire wouldn't work, so maybe we could use lightning, or ice?'

Swanhild finally smiled. 'You're thinking too basically,' she said. 'Subtlety would work better. Yes, we could hurl icicles at them, but it would take a lot of energy, and imagine if there were a whole flock of them.'

Rutger chewed on his knuckle. 'Oh, yes. What, then? Those are the only kinds of magic I really know how to use. You said you wouldn't teach me anything else until you were sure I could be trusted to use it properly.'

'That's true,' said Swanhild.

He smiled sideways at her. 'Do you trust me now, then?'

'Yes, I do,' said Swanhild. 'You know I do. And the time has come. But ... it won't be pleasant.'

'I would be learning how to kill things,' said Rutger. 'I wouldn't expect that to be pleasant.'

'No, I suppose not,' said Swanhild. 'Fine. At the next farm, buy a goose.'

*

The goose stood by the fire, honking irritably and trying to untangle itself from the piece of string Rutger had used to tether it to a stake. Rutger and Swanhild sat out of reach of its beak, Rutger's stomach already twisting in anticipation. They had set up camp by the river, at a safe distance from the nearby farm where they had bought the goose. Small, subtle spells like those they were about to cast wouldn't draw any attention. The more delicate forms of magic, Swanhild had explained, were often invisible.

'All right,' Rutger said eventually. 'What do I do? I'm already imagining it's a dragon,' he added.

Swanhild indicated the goose's fluttering grey wings. 'On a dragon, this is one of the most dangerous parts,' she said. 'The wings keep it out of your reach and allow it to attack from above before you have time to even see it coming. The other most dangerous thing is its fire, of course. But first we should learn how to stop it from flying. If you can disable a dragon in the air, it will fall to its death like any other flying creature.'

'Then how do we do that?' asked Rutger.

'The same way you would with a bird,' said Swanhild. 'Break its wing. A hard blow to the right place can shatter the bone in an instant.'

Rutger grimaced. 'Not fire, then — just force?'

'Yes,' said Swanhild. 'Watch me.' She made a short, jerking motion with her hand, and a puff of dust rose from the ground as if a rock had just landed there. 'You try it.'

Rutger looked away from the angry goose, pointed his palm at the ground, and closed his eyes while he focused on his magic. He channelled it to his hand and held it there for a while as he tried to point it in a different direction — away from fire, ice or lightning. But what else was there? What force was there that couldn't be seen, but still had enough power to shatter bone? Nothing occurred to him. He opened his eyes and released his magic in a quick burst. A dense blue fireball hit the ground with a faint *thud*.

'*Verdammt!*' Rutger rubbed his hand. 'I didn't mean to do that.'

'Never mind,' said Swanhild. 'Try again. Try harder.'

'But I need to understand what it is,' said Rutger. 'What the force is that you used. Something powerful but invisible. What is it?'

'I ... I don't know,' said Swanhild, looking puzzled for once. 'It's just force. I never thought about it.'

'But it's *not* just force!' said Rutger. 'It's a *kind* of force. Something you can feel but not see. Do you know what I mean?'

Swanhild frowned. 'You mean ... like the wind?'

'Yes!' Rutger sat bolt upright. 'Yes, that's it! That's what you used. It was air!' He was too excited to wait for Swanhild's reply: he quickly gathered some magic in his hand and prepared it — pushing it away from fire, away from water, and toward air. He released it with a short, sharp gesture just as Swanhild had done, and an invisible bolt of force shot from his palm and slammed into the ground, cracking it open. 'Yes!'

'Well done!' said Swanhild.

Rutger did it again. It worked perfectly. Even more excited now, he turned his new ability toward the fire, blowing the flames this way and that with swirling gestures from both hands. His ambitions were already soaring; there was no end to what he could do with this. Lift and carry objects, blast enemies away from himself, topple trees. Or maybe, he thought suddenly, maybe he could even use it to fly.

He was only just aware that Swanhild was speaking, and she had to repeat herself before he heard her properly. 'What's that?'

'Before you get carried away, you should try it on the goose,' she told him. 'I'll hold it still for you.'

Rutger's excitement vanished. 'Do we have to do this?'

'Yes,' Swanhild said flatly.

He watched the goose, which was now rooting at the ground for food. 'But it's cruel,' he said. 'Couldn't we at least kill it first?'

'No we can't,' said Swanhild. 'Listen. You're learning this so you can use it to kill. Killing means causing pain and suffering, even if it's to an enemy. Would you look at a ravening dragon, or an attacking Jünger, and say "I can't fight back; it would be cruel"?'

'Of course not, but that goose isn't attacking me,' said Rutger. 'It's just an animal.'

'Even so, if you want to learn how to break a wing, then you will have to do it with a wing that moves,' said Swanhild. 'A dragon won't hold still for you, and neither will this goose. We can kill it immediately afterwards.'

'But we'd be torturing it,' said Rutger. 'I won't do it.'

'We are going to war, Rutger,' said Swanhild. 'War is cruel. Even with your powers, if you can't find the will to cause pain and suffering, you won't last long. And you need to learn this if you want to survive.'

Rutger hesitated.

'Now,' said Swanhild, 'it's time.' She made a gesture, and the goose lifted into the air. Its wings opened instinctively and it began to flap, hanging helplessly in mid-air. 'Now, strike!' Swanhild said. 'Aim for the middle of the bone between the elbow and shoulder joints. Don't think, just do it!'

Disgust filled Rutger, but he didn't hesitate any longer. He gritted his teeth and shot a bolt of wind at the wing, aiming just where Swanhild had told him to. He heard the bone snap, and the goose shrieked. Its wing buckled and flailed in agony, hopelessly bent. But Swanhild wasn't done yet. She turned the goose in the air, pointing its other wing toward him. 'Again!'

Rutger struck again, breaking the other wing in a slightly different spot this time. The goose screamed again. Unable to take the sound, Rutger hit the animal a third time — this time in the throat. Its neck broke, and the goose died instantly.

Swanhild let its body drop. 'You did well,' she said. 'Of course, with a dragon you will have to strike harder.'

'Next time I'm going to aim for the neck first,' Rutger muttered.

Swanhild pulled the goose toward herself and started to pluck it. 'The wings are an easier target,' she said. 'Now, how does roast goose for dinner sound?'

'We don't have an oven—' Rutger started to say. He paused, and half-laughed. 'Never mind.'

Chapter 10

After that, Rutger practised his new skill every night when he could get the privacy. Fortunately, Swanhild didn't force him to practise on another live goose, so he used sticks instead; small ones at first, but slowly moving onto bigger and thicker ones which took more effort to break. At Swanhild's suggestion he used green wood, which would act more like bone, and once he had graduated to branches about as thick as a dragon's wingbone he started increasing the distance as well.

During this time they travelled out of the farmlands they had grown used to and moved on into wilder country, where there were fewer people. Forest appeared on the other side of the river in place of fields, and they took to camping under the trees every night. Now that they had the seclusion they needed, they took the next step in Rutger's lessons. Once he had found a suitable branch, Swanhild would use her magic to move it around and he would have to try to hit it. It was much harder with a moving target, and Swanhild liked to challenge him, throwing the branch around as unpredictably as she could manage, and once even tossing it straight at his face. He just managed to save himself from that one, hitting it just in time to shatter it before it bashed him on the head.

'That was a dirty trick!' he complained afterwards, though good-naturedly.

'But an attacking dragon will do exactly that,' said Swanhild. 'You don't think they'll give you a chance by keeping their distance, do you? No, they'll come straight at you like an arrow.' She made a swooping motion with her hand to demonstrate.

'I suppose so,' said Rutger. 'But I don't know if I'll have the courage to do that with a real dragon.'

'You will,' said Swanhild. 'And anyway, in a dangerous situation there's no room for courage. You react to survive. Fight, or run away.'

Nearby the deer watched placidly. As Rutger had hoped, they had become used to witnessing magic, and didn't react much to it anymore.

'I might run away,' he said. 'And so might they. I should see if I can do it on deerback.'

'Well, sometimes it's better to run than to fight,' said Swanhild. 'But yes, we should both try that.' She patted her deer on the nose. 'Poor deer; they carry us and put up with all our strange business, and never complain!'

'I'm sure they would if they could talk,' said Rutger. 'But maybe not; nobody is more patient than a deer.'

'And nothing is more fiery or savage than a dragon,' said Swanhild.

They fell silent, most likely both thinking of the dangers that might await them in the mountains. They would enter them soon. And there, thought Rutger, his first fight might come at last.

*

Not long after this, the road finally parted ways with the River Vent and wound on and up into the mountains, becoming narrower and more rutted. Not many people came this way anymore. They had once, when Drucht Valley was still occupied by its original inhabitants and the towns and villages there had traded with those on the other side of the mountains. But now the Jüngen controlled the cities at the end of that road, and they would never trade with the Gottlosen. And the mountains themselves were almost certainly patrolled by dragons.

'It should take us three days, maybe, to cross the mountains,' said Swanhild. 'On the way we should take turns to sleep at night, so someone can keep watch. Dragons can see in the dark, and we don't want to be ambushed.'

The mountains themselves were smaller than Rutger had expected. The hills of Schwartz Forest travelled north-east through Wendland and became mountains at this point, but to him they only looked like slightly larger and more rugged cousins. There wasn't even any snow at their peaks.

'They get bigger further along,' said Swanhild, seeing his disappointment. 'And the Drachengott's mountain is at the very end, where the two ranges meet. It's the biggest mountain in Wendland; just seeing it would thrill you.'

'Have you seen it, then?' asked Rutger.

'Yes, I have,' said Swanhild. 'Only once, but I'll never forget it.'

Rutger looked over at her as they rode along. 'I keep thinking I know you, but then you say something like that and I realise just how little I really do know,' he said.

'It takes a while to come to know someone completely,' said Swanhild. 'There are things about you I don't know.'

'Like what?' said Rutger.

'Well, how did your parents die?' said Swanhild.

'My mother died in childbirth, and my father died from a lung infection,' said Rutger. 'I was the seventh son out of fifteen children, but a lot of my brothers and sisters died while they were still young. That's normal enough. But what about you? Did you have any brothers? Sisters? What about your parents?'

'I had no family,' said Swanhild. 'Or none that I remember. I've ...' She hesitated, glancing away from him for a moment. 'I've always been alone, for as long as I can remember.'

'You were an orphan?' said Rutger.

'Yes,' said Swanhild. 'I grew up with nobody, and had to take care of myself.'

'That's so sad,' said Rutger. 'Even after my parents died, I still had my brothers and my sister to look after me. But you had no one at all?'

'No one,' said Swanhild. 'And after I lost my home, all I cared for was to take my revenge on the Drachengott. But I saw that I could not do it alone. I needed others to help me. And then I found you.'

'It was the same for me,' said Rutger. 'I didn't realise it until I met you, though.'

Swanhild gave him a knowing look. 'I think many things became clear when we met, Rutger von Gothendorf.'

His heart beat a little faster. 'Yes. Yes, they did.'

A long silence followed while they rode on. Rutger desperately wanted to say something else — anything to get rid of the sudden awkwardness between them — but nothing came to mind, and he silently cursed himself for being so bad with words. Instead he took in the scenery, hoping he would spot something they could talk about. The mountains might be dangerous, but they were beautiful in their own way; their sides dark with pine forest, their bare peaks jagged grey rock. The dirt road looked very pale by contrast, and, since by now it was completely deserted, the sound of the two deer's hooves sounded much louder. They had taken the bells off their antlers by now, not wanting to advertise their presence, and Rutger half missed their jangling. But in the silence of the mountains their cheerful din might have sounded hollow anyway.

'It's so quiet here,' he murmured, his former embarrassment forgotten.

'Good — we should be able to hear anyone coming from a long way,' said Swanhild.

Rutger nodded. 'We should watch the road as well as the sky.'

After all their preparations, he expected to see a dragon show up at any moment, but there was nothing. All he could see in the sky was the odd raven, and once an eagle so large that he almost mistook it for a dragon before he got a proper look at it. He wondered if he would hear one coming; if it would roar before it attacked. He remembered what that sounded like all too well: the screeching roar of the black dragon had come back to him in his dreams again and again.

'Listen!' Swanhild said suddenly, holding up a hand.

Rutger instinctively looked straight upward, but there was nothing in the sky. 'What is it?'

'There,' Swanhild pointed ahead. 'I hear hooves.'

A moment later Rutger heard them as well; the faint sound of oncoming deer. He tensed. 'What should we do?'

'They could be friendly,' said Swanhild. 'Let's meet them and find out — but be ready. If they attack us, none of them can be allowed to escape. None, you understand? The moment we use our magic, our secret will be out.'

Rutger's stomach turned. 'Maybe it would be better to run away.'

'Yes, maybe,' said Swanhild. 'So be careful. Even if things become threatening, hold yourself back from attacking them with magic. If they are Jüngen, let me do the talking. I might be able to fool them.'

'I'd rather do that than fight anyone,' said Rutger. 'I'll keep back.'

A short time later the strangers appeared around a bend in the road. There were more of them than Rutger had expected: a woman and three men, all on deerback. They were finely but practically dressed, in quality leather and cloth, and none of them were armed. But Rutger's heart sank the instant he saw the gemstones hanging around their necks. Each one was in a different kind of setting, but all of them looked expensive — gold and silver, one with other, smaller gemstones as decorations around the larger red one. The sapphire in Rutger's chest started to throb suddenly, as though it could sense the presence of other magic users. He said nothing, but gritted his teeth and channelled magic down both arms, holding it ready.

The four Jüngen had already spotted them. They reined in their deer, and one of the men held up a hand. 'Who are you?' he called. 'Faithful or unfaithful?'

'Faithful to the land and its gifts,' Swanhild answered immediately.

The Jüngen exchanged glances and then came on, slowly and cautiously. They stopped in front of Rutger and Swanhild, examining them. All four looked tense.

'What is your name?' the woman asked Swanhild.

'Ishild von Ketzergard,' she answered.

The four of them immediately relaxed. 'I know that name,' said the woman. 'Did you come here straight from Ketzergard?'

'No,' said Swanhild. 'I left the stronghold some time ago, to work as a free agent for my Lady Tanja. Are you going to join her?'

'Yes, we are,' said the woman. 'But where are you going?'

'To Drachenburg, as a spy,' said Swanhild. 'I am under orders to send back information on Lord Warin. Can you tell us anything about his doings lately?'

'Yes—' the woman began.

'Stop,' one of her companions cut her off. 'We can't share our information with anyone we meet.'

'Relax,' the woman told him. 'I know about this woman. She was in Drucht Valley before, and helped to recruit many people to the Ketzer. My contact mentioned her name as someone to trust.'

'Oh … well, then,' said the man. 'But who are *you*?' he added, looking at Rutger.

'This is my partner, Karl,' Swanhild answered for him. 'Assigned to help me in my mission.'

'Can't he speak for himself?' the man asked.

'Of course I can,' said Rutger. His mouth had gone dry, but he coughed and said; 'I came with Ishild to act as her bodyguard.'

The woman laughed. 'The famous Ishild hardly needs a bodyguard! I suppose Tanja sent you with her as a training mission?'

Swanhild smiled sweetly. 'Be nice to him — he's inexperienced but brave, and I trust him. But now, can you help us?'

'Yes, of course,' said the woman. 'But first, my name is Haedwig, and my friends here are Rolf, Frilo and Gosbert.' This last was the suspicious man who had questioned Rutger, but who now nodded pleasantly enough to him.

'Pleased to meet you,' said Rutger.

'The pleasure is mine as well,' said Swanhild. 'Are you returning to Ketzergard from a mission, or going to join Tanja?'

'We are new recruits,' said Haedwig. 'An agent in Drachenburg won us over to the cause, and finally gave us directions to an outpost on the other side of the mountains. From there, we'll be taken to Ketzergard. But come, we should eat together and share our information. I should tell you everything I can.'

'And I should give you information in return, to help you in Ketzergard,' said Swanhild.

'I would be very grateful,' said Haedwig. She turned her deer. 'Come, we passed a good sheltered spot not long ago.'

*

Haedwig directed them to a place further along the road, where a short pass led off the road to a clearing where they could sit down comfortably. Swanhild invited Rutger to light a fire, and he summoned it up without too much trouble, proud to be using magic in front of these people. Haedwig and her companions sat around it with him and Swanhild and shared some bread, leaving the deer to browse among the pines. It was a pleasant scene, but Rutger still felt nervous.

'What if a dragon finds us?' he asked.

'It won't be a danger to us,' said Rolf. 'So far as the dragons are concerned, the four of us are still faithful Jüngen. They'll ignore us if they see us, most likely. And if not, well, I think all of us together could deal with them easily enough.'

'You're high-ranking Jüngen, aren't you?' said Rutger, starting to relax around them now.

'Yes, we are,' said Rolf. 'Or we were. The Ketzer will welcome us with open arms; our powers are very highly trained.'

'If you're so powerful, why didn't one of you assassinate Warin?' Rutger asked, unable to stop himself.

'We would have liked to — it would have made the Ketzer trust us instantly,' said Haedwig. 'Unfortunately, not even all of us put together could have defeated a man like that.'

'So it's true?' said Swanhild. 'Warin has taken the final step?'

'Yes,' said Haedwig. 'The Drachengott was so pleased with his works in Drucht Valley that he gave Warin the greatest blessing.' Her jaw tightened. 'If only the Ketzer could have that power ...'

'The greatest blessing?' Rutger repeated. 'What does that mean?'

'It means that Warin takes his magic directly from the Drachengott himself,' said Gosbert. 'Which means his energies are all but inexhaustible. It's not a gift many worshippers are ever granted, but now Warin has it, no ordinary Jüngen or Ketzer could ever stand a chance of defeating him.'

'That leads me to the more important question,' said Swanhild, who didn't look at all surprised by the news. 'If Warin is so powerful, how are the Gottlosen still holding out against him in the valley? Nobody seems to know.'

'I don't know either,' said Haedwig. 'Nobody truly does. All we know is that the Gottlosen in Trutzberg have something on their side — some defence which can protect them against magic.'

'Interesting,' said Swanhild. 'But you know nothing more about it?'

'Only that Warin desperately wants to capture it,' said Haedwig. 'He sent out a message that anyone who brought this weapon to him would be given a fortune in gold and silver, and the blessing of the Drachengott himself. But if anyone in Trutzberg has tried to steal it, they failed.'

Swanhild nodded slowly, clearly deep in thought.

'Do you think the Ketzer would want this weapon?' Rutger asked.

'Oh, certainly,' said Haedwig. 'But to try to take it would be suicide, and magic would not help. The stories say that when Jüngen assassins tried to attack the Lord of Trutzberg, he killed every single one of them himself — using only the weapon. Not one Jünger ever survived an encounter with it, which is why we know so little about it.'

'Then why have they not attacked Warin directly?' asked Swanhild.

'I don't know,' said Haedwig. 'Perhaps Trutzberg's ruler is hoping to win concessions from Warin rather than kill him outright.'

'I will find out,' Swanhild said finally.

'Then good luck,' said Haedwig. 'But what about the Ketzer? Can you tell us more about them? Our contact gave very little away.'

'I can tell you that their numbers are growing,' said Swanhild. 'More and more Jüngen are defecting to their side the way you have. But Tanja's full intentions are unknown. Some think she plans to make an alliance with the Gottlosen, or with the Gallien king. But neither would ever fully trust her.'

'Well, what do *you* think she plans to do?' asked Rolf.

'I have my suspicions,' said Swanhild, 'but for now I will keep them to myself.'

Rutger listened to all this with fascination. Until now he had known almost nothing about the Ketzer; they were rebel Jüngen, that was all. But now it seemed the situation was a lot more complicated than that.

'Anyway,' Swanhild went on, 'if you can give me the name of your contact in Drachenburg, and information on how to reach him, I can give you the names of some of Tanja's high command. That should help you win their trust.'

'Thank you,' said Haedwig. 'Our contact was a man who called himself Egbert. He works in a tavern called the Twisted Lip; you'll recognise him by his enormous nose.'

Rolf and Frilo both chuckled.

Swanhild smiled. 'Good, that should be a big help to us. Now, the Ketzer. Tanja's right-hand man is named Franz, and he is her cousin. Some of her advisors are Nordemann, Gisila, and a Britainnien woman named Ethel. Mention them, and me, and it should help.'

'Excellent,' said Haedwig. 'We were very lucky to meet you.' She cast a satisfied look at her friends. 'We expect to climb the Ketzer hierarchy very quickly thanks to our level of power, and the sooner we can win their confidence the better.'

'Yes,' said Swanhild, 'the Ketzer are not naturally trusting. It took me a long time to win their trust myself.'

They chatted on for a while after that, discussing various things about Ketzer and Jüngen politics which Rutger listened to but found less interesting than they apparently did. He finished his bread and warmed his hands over the fire until Haedwig finally announced that she and her friends should be on their way. Rutger put the fire out by re-absorbing its energy, and the meeting broke up. They rode out back to the road together, and there parted ways.

'The next time you come to Ketzergard, be sure to come and see us,' said Haedwig.

'We will,' said Swanhild. 'Good luck.'

'And to the both of you,' said Rolf.

The four new Ketzer rode off the way Rutger and Swanhild had come, leaving the two of them to go on through the mountains.

'That was a lucky meeting,' Swanhild said, once they had gone. 'But I guessed they were likely to be defectors; Ketzergard is back that way.'

'You handled them well!' Rutger said admiringly. 'I had no idea you were so important.'

Swanhild laughed. 'The Ketzer only think I work for them, but I never truly have. Still, I help them when it suits me. Tanja made it clear that I wasn't welcome back, but she tolerates me because I sometimes send valuable information back to her.'

'And you use a different name with them,' said Rutger. 'Why?'

'To make it harder for anyone to track me, of course,' said Swanhild. 'I change my name as often as I need to.'

He frowned. 'Then Swanhild isn't your real name?'

'No,' she answered after a short pause. 'It's the name I use with you. Ishild is the name I use with Ketzer. And I have others for other places and other people.'

Rutger's frown deepened. 'But what's your real name?'

Swanhild smiled gently at him, clearly aware of his hurt feelings. 'Don't take it personally,' she said. 'Names are less important than people think. But one day I promise I will tell you my real name.'

'When?' he pressed.

'When the time is right,' said Swanhild. 'For now, we have to complete our journey. But I think our plans have changed.'

'I don't think we could fight Warin,' Rutger agreed. 'Not if he has infinite energy.'

'It would be a suicide mission to go up against him now,' said Swanhild. 'So we won't go to Drachenburg. Instead, we will go to Trutzberg. After all, it's the place where we can find the means to destroy Warin.'

Rutger's face slackened. 'You can't mean—?'

'But I do,' Swanhild said calmly. 'We are going to find this weapon, and take it for ourselves.'

Chapter 11

They travelled on uneventfully for the rest of that day, and camped that night in a hidden spot just off the path. Their supplies were running a little low, but Swanhild was confident that they would reach Drucht Valley soon.

Sure enough, by noon the next day they could see their destination. The road twisted ahead of them, curving between the mountains, but every now and then they could see between them to the wide, flat green expanse of Drucht Valley. The thin silver line of a river wound through it, and here and there dark spots marked the positions of towns and villages. The air had begun to feel warmer.

'We'll be there soon,' said Swanhild.

'I hope we can find a place to stay,' said Rutger. 'It would be nice to sleep in a bed again.'

'Then let's not waste time!' Swanhild said cheerfully. 'Come on!' She kicked her deer in the ribs, and the animal sped up.

But here, closer to the valley, something else had changed. Rutger kept watching the sky, and now he started to see something new. Dark shapes, circling high above, their outlines vague at this distance, but still clear enough to tell him that these weren't birds. He put a hand on the hilt of his sword, mostly out of habit, and swore softly. 'Dragons!'

Swanhild was looking upward as well. 'Yes, we have to hope they won't bother us.'

To Rutger's relief the dragons didn't seem interested in the two travellers. They stayed up in the sky, sometimes visible perching on ledges high up on the mountainsides, but none of them coming low enough to be more than distant presences. After a while he started to relax again. They were nearly out of the mountains now; the road started to slope downward, and at the base of the last mountain he could see a small town nestled amongst grassy foot-hills. They should be able to make it there before dark.

'We're close now!' he said, with real relief.

Beside him, Swanhild started to say something, but then tensed and looked upward. Rutger followed her gaze, and swore again. Above, a dark shape had detached itself from the side of a mountain and begun to fly down toward them in a slow dive, its wings angled backward and neck outstretched. Heart pounding, Rutger let go of his deer's reins with one hand and prepared his magic.

Beside him, Swanhild did the same. 'Don't attack unless it strikes first,' she said urgently. 'It might just want to question us.'

The dragon stopped its descent a short way above the shying deer. Flapping hard to stay in place, it stared down at Rutger and Swanhild through narrow golden eyes. Its scales were dark brown, its wing membranes yellow, and the smell that came off it brought a rush of panicked memories back to Rutger. That stench like hot metal. He froze to the spot, aware of almost nothing else but the rush of magic up and down his arm.

'What do you want?' Swanhild shouted boldly.

The dragon's eyes narrowed even further, and then a voice spoke from out of the air – a growling, male voice. *Where are you going, humans?*

'To Drachenburg, to serve Lord Warin,' said Swanhild. 'We are both Jüngen.'

But I see no stones, the dragon hissed.

'We took them off, to avoid attention,' said Swanhild.

Or perhaps you took them off because you are traitors, said the dragon. He started to snarl. *Ketzer scum! You came here from Ketzergard — confess it!* Yellow fire began to flicker between his teeth.

'We did not,' said Swanhild. 'In the Drachengott's name, leave us in peace.'

But the mention of the Drachengott only seemed to provoke the dragon. He roared and dropped out of the sky, coming straight at them with his mouth open to spit flame.

'*Now!*' Swanhild yelled. She sent a bolt of silver light straight at the dragon, hitting him in his open mouth. Instantly the flames vanished, but he spread his talons and descended on Swanhild and her deer. The animal bucked wildly as the dragon latched onto it, sinking his talons into the poor creature's neck and chest. Clinging on, the dragon lashed out at Swanhild with his darting head, jaws snapping for her.

Rutger's own steed panicked and bolted, throwing him out of the saddle. He landed hard on his back, but instinct made him get up before he had even registered the pain. Swanhild's deer was darting in circles, bellowing in terror, and only its antlers had stopped the dragon from biting Swanhild in half. She lashed out with magic, but missed. 'Help me!'

Rutger's frozen panic only lasted a moment. He raised his hands and sent a bolt of wind straight at the dragon's flailing wings. It struck one of them, and the crunch of breaking bone was followed by an unearthly scream.

The dragon let go of Swanhild's deer and fell onto the road, one wing bent at an unnatural angle. Silvery blood spattered onto the road, hissing and steaming in the dust. Freed, the deer threw Swanhild off and fled.

Rutger ran to her and grabbed her by the elbow, lifting her to her feet. She stood, groaning. 'Quickly,' she said. 'Before he recovers.'

The dragon was up now, hissing in agony. *Traitors! Heretics!*

'Kill him,' said Swanhild, pulling her arm out of Rutger's grip. 'Kill him now. Do it!'

Rutger channelled more magic to his hands and struck wildly, but in his panic he instinctively reverted to the first kind of magic he had learned. Blue fire enveloped the dragon, hiding it from view as it came on at him.

'No—!' Swanhild started to shout, but she never finished. The dragon lunged straight through Rutger's fire and hit him head-on. He felt a hard blow to his chest, over the scar, and then he was down and the dragon was on him, its jaws closing around his neck and shoulder. Blood welled up in Rutger's mouth as he tried to cry out. He felt his skin split as the talons sank into his chest and right arm, and then the dragon pulled back with his jaws and began to shake violently, savaging him like a dog with a rabbit.

But Rutger wasn't dead yet. And his left arm was still free. With a last, desperate effort, he blasted all the magic he could summon out of his chest, down his arm and out through his hand. Not fire this time, but ice. He felt the impact slam through the dragon's body and into his, and immediately the jaws relaxed their grip. The dragon rolled off him, and Rutger dragged himself away. He tried to get up, right arm raised to attack again, but then he saw it. The dragon, lying in the middle of the road, impaled by an icicle the size of a spear. The ice was already melting, but it had done its job, and as the water trickled onto the ground it quickly turned silver with the rush of hot blood that followed. The dragon's yellow eyes had gone dim. They stared sightlessly at their killer, and then the beast slumped onto the road.

Rutger stared back, right hand still raised. He couldn't seem to lift it any higher; it felt hot and heavy, and something wet was trickling down his chest. He looked down at himself and saw the blood soaking into his shirt.

'Swanhild, I think I'm hurt,' he said, and as he tried to reach for the deep fang marks on his throat his strength suddenly drained out of him, and he toppled backward.

He didn't feel himself hit the ground. Nor did he really see anything much. The world had gone dim and grey. But he did hear Swanhild's scream.

'*NO!*'

He felt her hands on him, clutching at him, pulling his shirt open to expose the wounds. She felt just as warm as always, but he felt so cold now. All the sensation seemed to be fading out of his body. His eyes were going dark.

But even as the blackness closed over his head, a light appeared. Bright, silvery light. It showed him Swanhild's beautiful face, looking down on him as if hovering in the sky. But her expression had changed it almost out of recognition. Savage desperation twisted her mouth into a snarl, and as Rutger finally lost consciousness he thought he saw those eyes, those strange reddish eyes, change. Blazing red, the pupils slitted, glaring out of a face where they did not belong at all.

Chapter 12

When Rutger woke up he felt fine — but not for long. He lay with his eyes closed, enveloped by peaceful warmth, only just aware of his own body. But the moment he opened his eyes and tried to move, the pain hit him. He gasped and fell back, his head spinning. A savage ache had left his neck rigid, and his right arm felt stiff and useless. 'Swanhild ...' he groaned her name.

A warm hand touched him on the forehead. 'It's all right. Just lie still.'

Rutger looked around from his prone position, and realised that he was indoors. A wooden-plank ceiling was above him, and he was on a bed. Swanhild was there, offering him a mug of water.

'Here, drink this,' she said.

Rutger managed to swallow it, and started to feel a little better. 'What happened ... ?'

'You're hurt, but you will recover,' said Swanhild. 'I brought you here. We're in Jarlsberg, just beyond the mountains.'

Rutger lay still, letting the memories of what had happened slowly wash over him. 'That dragon ... I killed him. But he ...'

'Yes, you did,' said Swanhild. 'And I thought ...'

Rutger turned his head toward her, and saw how pale she looked. Her eyes were hollow and her hair lank, and there was a slight tremble in her hands.

'Are you all right?' he asked, suddenly worried.

She smiled weakly. 'I'll be fine.'

'You healed me,' said Rutger. 'Didn't you? I felt your magic — I saw it. I would have died if you hadn't ...'

'Yes,' said Swanhild. 'Yes, you would have died. For a little while I thought you had. How do you feel?'

'My neck hurts, and my arm,' said Rutger. 'But—' He looked straight at her. 'You saved my life, Swanhild.'

'I had to,' she answered. 'I couldn't let you die.'

He managed to smile. 'How can I ever repay you?'

'You don't have to,' said Swanhild. 'Just rest and get well: the healing spell I used on you should finish its work by the morning, and you'll be able to get up. You should be back to your full strength in a day or so.'

Rutger carefully reached up to touch his neck with his left hand. The skin felt swollen around his throat and shoulder, but the pain didn't flare up when he touched the wounds. They had already sealed over, and the pain was deep inside. 'I didn't know magic could heal,' he said. 'Why didn't you teach me that?'

'Because it's too dangerous,' said Swanhild. 'Only the most advanced magic users can use magic to heal wounds, and even then they rarely do it. The amount of energy it takes can kill you very easily.'

Once again, Rutger noticed how sick she looked. 'You risked your own life to save mine.'

'Yes,' said Swanhild. 'But I'll be fine; I just need a little time to recover.'

He lay back, head spinning. 'You shouldn't do that again.'

'If the alternative is your death, I would do it again in a heartbeat,' Swanhild said fiercely. 'Now that's enough. Get some sleep, and everything will be fine.'

Rutger wanted to argue with her, but he didn't, and not only because he was exhausted and still weak. The ferocity with which she had said that she would happily risk her own death for his sake put a warmth into his heart which went far deeper than her magic ever could have, and it soothed his fears and helped him to relax. He lay back, feeling safe at last, and let himself sleep.

*

The next day Rutger woke up feeling much better. The pain had died down, and his neck and shoulder only twinged a little as he sat up in bed. Morning sunlight was coming in through the window, and Swanhild was asleep in the other bed. The room she had found for the pair of them was small but clean, and there was a table between their beds with something on a plate with cloth draped over it. Rutger lifted the cloth and found a wedge of cheese, some dried sausage and a small loaf of bread underneath. The sight of the food made him realise just how hungry he was, and he sat on the edge of his bed and helped himself. Swallowing hurt a bit, but the food tasted so good that he could ignore the discomfort. While he ate, he carefully flexed his right arm. It was still a bit stiff, but he could use it again. Swanhild must have taken his blood-soaked shirt off him; he was bare-chested and could easily see the damage the dragon had done to him. Deep scars stood out on his sides, just below his ribcage, where the beast's talons had cut into him, and there were more scars on his elbow and upper arm. Of course he couldn't see his throat, but he could see some of the tooth marks on his shoulder and collarbone. Two rows of deep slash-marks, already forming into raised red scars like welts.

To his surprise, as he rubbed his thumb over the marks, he found he felt rather proud to have them. After all, how many people could say they had fought a dragon and lived to tell the tale? And how many people had scars like these to prove it? He had fought his first real battle, and he had won, even if it had almost killed him. But in the future, he promised himself, he wouldn't make the mistakes he had made this time. Next time he would strike first, and not let panic overwhelm him or push him into making stupid mistakes. He couldn't allow Swanhild to put herself in danger again, or let himself be injured this badly — and he wouldn't. He promised himself that.

Swanhild woke up while he was still eating. He watched her getting up, relieved to see that she looked much healthier now. The pallor had gone from her face, her hands had stopped shaking, and her smile toward him was stronger.

'Good morning,' she said. 'How do you feel?'

'Fine,' said Rutger. 'You?'

'Much stronger,' she said. 'But I shouldn't use any magic until I'm completely recovered. Hopefully, we won't need it. Can you move your arm?'

Rutger flexed it, wincing. 'It still hurts a bit, but yes.' He paused. 'What happened to our deer?'

'I managed to track them both down,' said Swanhild. 'Mine isn't too badly hurt. I put both of them in a stable; they should be cared for there. If you feel strong enough, we can go out into the town today and buy some supplies, and then we can plan our entry into Trutzberg.'

'I'm fine,' said Rutger. 'Here.' He pushed the plate of food toward her.

Swanhild picked up some cheese. 'We don't have too much money left,' she said. 'But we should have enough for some food. We need one other thing as well: dye, to hide the scars on our chests.'

'Will they check us when we go into Trutzberg, then?' asked Rutger.

'We should expect it, yes,' said Swanhild. 'They haven't survived this long by being stupid.'

'I know a dye that works well on skin,' said Rutger. 'I used it all the time back home. Deadleaf extract — I used to make it myself, for dyeing the hides. I always had to be careful not to get any on myself, because it took days to come off my skin.'

'That sounds good,' said Swanhild. 'Do you think you could find deadleaf here?'

'It's common enough,' said Rutger. 'The trick is knowing how to prepare it.'

'Then that's what we'll do,' Swanhild decided. 'And with any luck, this time we won't run into any more dragons.'

*

That afternoon, once they had gone on a shopping trip for more supplies, including a new shirt for Rutger to wear, they left Jarlsberg for a walk in the countryside beyond its walls. Both of them walked a little slowly now, but it wasn't a strenuous walk. A pleasant stretch of pine forest sat just to the west of Jarlsberg's walls, and they explored it at a leisurely pace until Rutger found the plant he was after; a small shrub with brown, curling leaves that looked dead even when newly grown. For some reason, the leaves of the deadleaf plant were only green when they first sprouted, and turned dull brown as soon as they had finished opening. The flowers which grew between the leaves were black and smelled sickly.

'It's an ugly plant,' Rutger agreed, 'but very useful. Keep away from the flowers, though: they're poisonous.'

Swanhild helped him gather some of the larger leaves, and back in the privacy of their room Rutger put them in a metal pot with some water and used magic to boil the mixture. It tired him out, but it was a useful exercise in controlling the flow of his magic, and after a while the mixture started to reduce and then thicken while Swanhild stirred it with a stick. Rutger watched it closely until the consistency was just right, and then shut off his magic. The bubbling stopped, and both of them inspected the thick, dark brown liquid.

'Perfect,' said Rutger. 'Now let's see if it works.' He pulled his shirt off with some difficulty, and picked up a rag which he dipped into the dye. It was still hot, and he gingerly rubbed it over the scar in the middle of his chest. Just as he had hoped, a leathery brown stain spread over his skin, darkening the scar until it nearly matched the rest of his skin. He blew on it to make it dry faster, and critically examined the results.

'What do you think?' he asked Swanhild.

'It's a very close match,' she said. 'It should work as long as nobody looks too closely. But it won't work as well on me; my skin is too pale.'

'Damn.' Rutger chewed on his thumbnail while he thought it over. 'You couldn't rub it over your whole body, could you?' he asked, thinking it was a stupid idea even as he suggested it.

Swanhild, however, frowned thoughtfully. 'It could be worth a try. But I'll need some privacy.'

'Of course.' Rutger stood up. 'I'll go outside — call me when you're ready.'

He left the room, resisting the temptation to look back at Swanhild as she started to strip off her clothes.

Outside, he leaned against the wall and idly fingered the scars on his neck, which was a habit he had fallen into, and tried not to imagine Swanhild naked — which of course he failed at. He grimaced to himself. It would be so easy to say something to her, if he could only bring himself to do it. But, of course, he couldn't.

A short time later, Swanhild's muffled voice came from inside. 'I'm finished.'

Rutger cautiously opened the door, and found her fully clothed. But now her pale skin had turned light brown. It was much more convincing than he had expected.

He couldn't help it: he laughed. 'Hah, look at you!' he said. 'You're tanned!'

Swanhild laughed, too. 'Yes, it looks as though I am. Just like one of your pelts. I don't look silly, do I?'

'No, not at all,' said Rutger. 'In fact you don't stand out as much now. You look more like a commoner. Your pale skin made you look like a noblewoman.'

'Oh,' said Swanhild. 'I never thought of that. But here ...' She pulled the front of her dress down, careful not to expose anything other than the scar between her breasts. 'Is it hidden now?'

Rutger tried not to seem too interested in looking at her chest, but he nodded. 'It's almost invisible.'

'Perfect.' Swanhild covered herself up again. 'Your plan was a good one. Now we have to see if it convinces the guards at Trutzberg.'

'And if it doesn't?' said Rutger.

'Then we'll have to tell them we're Ketzer and hope that makes them more sympathetic,' said Swanhild. 'Or we fight our way out, which would not be a good start.'

'They'll kill us if they think we're Jüngen, won't they?' said Rutger.

'Almost certainly, yes,' said Swanhild. 'But Ketzer might be another matter. The Ketzer have no alliance to Trutzberg, but they aren't enemies either.'

'It's a shame they can't work together,' said Rutger, sitting down and pouring himself a drink. He offered Swanhild a cup, and she accepted it and sat down beside him.

'Yes, it is a pity,' she agreed. 'But the Ketzer have no real interest in helping the Gottlosen. They like the power the Drachengott gave them, but want to use it for themselves rather than obey him. They may even hope to take over Wendland for their own purposes, although they could never do that while the Drachengott is still alive. If they did ever ally with the Gottlosen, it would be for their own benefit and no other reason. But if we can get our hands on this weapon that the Lord of Trutzberg has, we could change the balance of power in Wendland for good.'

'If we took it, we'd leave Trutzberg defenceless,' said Rutger.

'Not if we used it to kill Warin,' said Swanhild. 'Trutzberg's ruler might be holding back, but we would not. In any case, once we infiltrate the city we can find out what his intentions are, and change our plans then if needs be. For all we know, he does have a good reason.'

'And if we do decide to take the weapon, we'll have to come up with a plan for that as well,' said Rutger. 'One that won't get us killed, I hope.'

'Yes,' said Swanhild. 'That would be a good start.'

Chapter 13

They left Jarlsberg the next morning, carrying an extra supply of deadleaf just in case, and rode the short distance to Trutzberg along a paved road which had plenty of other traffic on it. Swanhild's deer now had a slight limp in one foreleg, and the poor animal's neck and shoulders were badly scarred by the dragon's attack, but, as she had said, the damage wasn't too bad. The deer should recover, given enough rest. Swanhild was careful to ride slowly, and Rutger followed suit. If the deer died, they wouldn't be able to afford a replacement.

Drucht Valley looked a lot more peaceful than Rutger had expected. The other travellers along the road to Trutzberg, mostly traders by the look of them, sat on their deer or up on their carts without any apparent fear or concern, often travelling alongside each other so they could enjoy a chat. The landscape on either side of the road was quiet and green, and there were no dragons visible in the sky. It could have been anywhere in the country, and easily a place far away from any

Jüngen influence. Maybe Warin and the ruler of Trutzberg were under some kind of truce to keep dragons and Jüngen away?

But if that was the case, the city of Trutzberg itself still had plenty of security on display. The city had been built on a large hilltop, with its ruler's castle easily visible at the centre — high stone walls flying a yellow banner with some emblem on it which Rutger couldn't see at that distance. The rest of the city looked as though it was mostly stone as well, but a good part of it was invisible behind the fortifications; high, thick stone walls topped with spikes, whose gates were open but watched over by a squad of about twenty well-armed and alert guards. Everyone who went into the city had to stop and present some papers, which were closely examined before the holders were allowed in. Those who had no papers were ushered through a door just inside the gates.

'Ah, there we are,' said Swanhild. 'Either we show them papers, or we go in there to be questioned. Do you want to continue?'

'Yes,' said Rutger. 'We don't have any other choice. Anyway, we already have our story ready: we're here to find a new home together.'

'We certainly are, Karlchen,' said Swanhild.

He smiled. 'And you, Heikchen.'

They pressed on through the gate, and dismounted before approaching the guards. The man who appeared to be in charge held out a hand. 'Papers?'

'We don't have any,' said Rutger, vaguely aware of the sweat beading on his forehead.

'That way,' the man said shortly, pointing to the office door. 'We'll hold onto your deer.'

Rutger silently handed the reins to a guard, and he and Swanhild let themselves be escorted through the door into what did indeed turn out to be an office. It looked simple enough inside: a long desk with a couple of chairs, a cabinet with a few papers poking out of a drawer, and a patient-looking middle aged man waiting for them. But Rutger couldn't ignore the pair of armed guards who were posted just inside the door, and who moved to quietly close it the moment he and Swanhild were inside. If anything went wrong, escaping would almost certainly mean being forced to kill. Rutger's mouth went dry, and his scars throbbed.

The man behind the desk waved to them. 'First things first,' he said. 'Show me your chests.'

Rutger glanced quickly at Swanhild. She looked perfectly calm. The dye had now settled into her skin and looked more natural than before, although it was still odd to see her look like a tanned country woman.

'I'll go first,' she said after a pause, and reached up to unlace the front of her dress. As before she only bared the scar and left her breasts covered, while the official got up to inspect her. He peered closely at the skin over her breastbone, then reached out and roughly pulled her dress open all the way, exposing her entire chest.

'Hey—!' Rutger protested.

Swanhild said nothing, but she flushed as the man examined her, prodding and poking her as if she was a cow in the marketplace and he was checking her for ticks. The sight of her being treated so offhandedly aggravated Rutger so much that he couldn't help himself. 'Take your hands off her,' he growled.

The official looked up, but before he could answer Swanhild said; 'It's all right, Karl. This needs to be done. Please forgive my fiancé,' she added, to the official, 'he can be overprotective.'

Thankfully, the man cracked a smile. 'It's fine, we're finished,' he said, letting go of her. Swanhild laced up her dress again, and Rutger hid a sigh of relief. He pulled off his shirt and let the man check his own chest. But, although there was a slight pit in the skin where the sapphire had entered him, the dye hid any discolouration, and after a short inspection the official nodded.

'That's all fine,' he said. 'Now please sit down.'

Rutger pulled his shirt back on, heart fluttering, and sat on one of the chairs provided.

'What was all that about?' he asked, trying to sound indignant and succeeding at it; he was absolutely certain it hadn't been at all necessary to make Swanhild show her breasts. This old pervert probably just enjoyed it.

'We need to make certain no Jüngen make their way into the city,' said the man, unmoved. 'Some have marks on their chests: scars, or tattoos to hide those scars. It's not so much of a risk these days, but we have to be careful. Now then, why don't you tell me who you both are?' As he spoke, he pulled a couple of papers toward himself and picked up a pen. Holding it ready, he looked up enquiringly at the two of them.

'My name is Heike and this is Karl,' said Swanhild. 'We both came from Bonndorf, but now we want to begin a new life together here in Trutzberg.'

The man raised an eyebrow. 'That's a risky thing to do, moving here so close to Jüngen territory.'

'Oh, but we heard Trutzberg was safe,' said Swanhild, with a convincing show of surprise. 'So well protected that even Lord Warin had agreed to leave it in peace.'

'That may be, for now,' the man said darkly. 'But some would still call you reckless. Still, that's none of my concern.' He scribbled something down. 'What are your professions?'

'I'm a tanner,' Rutger said truthfully. 'I cure leather and sew it as well — I made that coat Heike is wearing.'

The man looked at Swanhild. 'Fine work,' he said. 'You should see if you can find a job with the city guard; they always need leather goods.'

'I will — thank you,' said Rutger.

'And you?' said the man, speaking to Swanhild. 'Do you have a trade?'

'I'm a jeweller,' said Swanhild, surprising Rutger. She smiled. 'I can do almost anything with a precious stone and some silver.'

The man wrote some more. 'With useful trades like that, you should do well enough. Still, I'm curious. You're both from Bonndorf. Why not live there? Why come all the way here and leave your friends and family behind?'

Rutger took Swanhild's hand. 'I didn't want to leave them,' he said honestly, 'but my Heike always wanted to live here.'

'So you let her drag you away from your home?' asked the man. He was probing now, putting pressure on them to make them give themselves away as liars; Rutger was sure of it.

He thought quickly, and before Swanhild could step in he said; 'Yes, I did. It was hard, but I couldn't bear to be parted from her.' He gave her hand a squeeze. 'I love her, and I would die for her. Leaving my home was a small price to pay, to be with her.' He heard the passion in his own voice, and a strange warmth spread through his chest like hot wine. He smiled foolishly, and almost immediately started to feel embarrassed, but relieved as well. He had said how he felt out loud, no matter what the reason for doing so had been.

And it worked. The official laughed. 'Your betrothed is head over heels for you,' he told Swanhild. 'You can wrap him around your fingers for as long as you keep him that way — my wife would envy you! If only that magic could last.' He picked up a candle, dripped some wax onto the two sheets and stamped them with a seal before pushing them across the desk. 'Here,' he said. 'Your papers. From now on you can come in and out of the city as long as the gates are open and you have these ready to show the guards.'

Rutger took his. 'Thank you,' he said, face burning.

'You're welcome,' said the man. 'Now, off you go, both of you.'

They left the office together, and found their deer waiting in the hands of the guards.

'This one's in bad shape,' said one, giving Swanhild back the reins. 'You should find someone to treat those wounds. What was it, a bear attack?'

'I don't know,' Swanhild smoothly lied. 'He got loose during the night, and we found him injured. Thank you for taking care of him.'

The guard nodded. 'Welcome to Trutzberg, both of you.'

Rutger took his deer's reins back, and he and Swanhild entered the city, side by side like the lovers he wished they could be. All he could think of was what he had said in the office, his own words repeating themselves in his head. Even the fact that they had successfully bluffed their way into the city seemed less important beside it.

But if Swanhild was thinking of it, she didn't show it. She frowned as they walked along, the deers' hooves clattering on the cobbled street. 'That was too easy,' she said.

'He questioned us pretty closely,' said Rutger.

'I don't mean that part,' said Swanhild. 'I meant our scars. A brief look by one man was all it took: if he was an expert he would have done more than look and take a quick poke at us. They don't seem so worried about Jünger infiltrators. That tells me they don't expect to be attacked, so perhaps they do have a treaty with Warin. Or this weapon makes them so confident that they don't believe any Jünger would dare come into Trutzberg at all. We need to find out more.'

'I suppose we can just ask around,' said Rutger. 'While we find a place to stay and a stable for the deer.'

'Yes,' said Swanhild. 'Once we have the deer stabled and have hired a room, let's split up and explore. Talk to everyone we meet. Then we can eat together tonight, and share our information. What do you think?'

'Good idea,' said Rutger. 'It would be interesting to see the city as well. Have you ever been in a city before?' he added.

'Yes, but not often,' said Swanhild. 'I prefer quieter places. All these people make me nervous.'

There certainly were a lot of people around. Rutger took in their surroundings with fascination. The streets here were paved, with stone gutters on either side. The houses looked bigger and older, and there were more of them, packed together so tightly that there was hardly any space between them at all. There was hardly any space between the people either, for that matter. It was lucky that Rutger and Swanhild had their deer with them; they helped to clear the way. Even so, they started to be jostled almost as soon as they were in the city proper. Rutger's ears were full of the babble of voices, and the smell of sweat and hair was overpowering. He couldn't blame Swanhild for not liking it here too much; he could see how nervy she looked – a little like the deer she was leading, in fact.

Fortunately they were able to find a place for both animals not far from the gates. A large stable had room for them, and the owner promised that she could treat the injured deer as well. Rutger handed over enough money to keep both animals fed and sheltered for a week, and he and Swanhild shouldered the saddlebags before setting out to find an inn.

'I recommend the Dead Dragon on Ring Street,' the stable owner told them. 'The food is very good.'

'What a terrible name for an inn,' Swanhild said as they left.

'Oh, I don't know.' Rutger touched the handle of his sword, which he had sensibly left packed away during their interrogation. 'I would call a dead dragon a good thing.'

Swanhild's lip curled. 'How charming, taking pleasure in dead things.'

'But dragons are evil!' Rutger exclaimed.

'Evil — or used,' said Swanhild. 'Who are you to judge?'

'A dragon killed my brother,' he said, angry with her for the first time. 'Two of them have tried to kill me. You'll never persuade me they aren't evil. Anyway, you taught me how to kill them — what's got into you now?'

Swanhild hesitated, then gave him a forced kind of smile. 'Forgive me,' she said, 'I get irritable when I'm nervous. Let's go and look at this inn.'

'It's fine,' said Rutger, although he felt anything but. He had seen the quick flash of rage in her red-brown eyes, and it had disturbed him. He knew he had said something that had genuinely upset her, but he wasn't sure what. A mixture of guilt and resentment sat in his stomach, and he couldn't bring himself to apologise.

They found the Dead Dragon in any case — the sign did indeed have a picture of a dead dragon, lying on its back with a sword sticking out of its belly.

Swanhild gave it a cursory glance. 'That would upset any Jünger who saw it,' she said stiffly. 'Maybe they put it there to catch out any spies who came this way.'

'Listen, if you don't like it—' Rutger began.

Swanhild ignored him and went inside. He followed, the saddlebags chafing his sore shoulder. Inside, the inn was fairly well-lit, and boasted a large fireplace at one end. Behind the bar, a burly woman was busy serving food and drinks to a good number of customers, who sat at small tables placed here and there, or stood leaning against the walls while they chatted. The place smelled of smoke and roasting meat.

'Well, if this is the inside of a dead dragon it's nicer than I expected,' said Rutger, hoping to lighten things up.

Swanhild, though, ignored him. She went over to the bar and spoke briefly to the woman, who pointed her toward a man who was busy throwing another log on the fire. Swanhild pushed past a couple of drunks to get to him. Rutger kept back, staying near the door and waiting for her to return. She talked briefly to the man, and gave him some money before coming back to Rutger.

'I've hired us a room for the night,' she said. 'We have to pay again in the morning if we want to stay another night. Come on.'

They went through a door at the far end of the inn, and into a small and fairly basic room. It had a pair of beds, a cupboard and a rug on the floor, and that was it. But there was at least a glass window, which impressed Rutger; glass was expensive.

He gratefully dumped his bags on the nearest bed, but kept his sword and money bag with him.

'You won't need that,' said Swanhild, looking at the sword.

'I know, but I like to keep it with me,' said Rutger.

Swanhild looked as though she was about to say something else, but she only gave a quick nod and said, 'Fine. I'll see you here tonight. Don't do anything stupid.' She dropped a key on the bed and walked out.

'Swanhild—' Rutger began, but she didn't turn back, and he didn't want to chase after her like a small boy afraid of losing his mother. He let her go, and gloomily stuffed the key into his pocket. He had been looking forward to exploring the city, but their argument had spoiled his mood.

Still, there was no point in wasting time moping here. He took a piece of dried meat out of the saddlebag nearest to him, and left too. Outside, Swanhild had already left the inn. He felt a curious sense of loss not to see her there waiting for him.

Chapter 14

Rutger might have begun his exploration in a low mood, but it didn't take long to lift. There was too much to see and do out in the city for him to dwell on Swanhild's sudden coldness toward him. Ring Street was right in the centre of Trutzberg, and it was indeed ring-shaped. In fact, as he discovered, it went right around the castle where the city's ruler must live. The castle itself was unlike any building he had seen before: great round towers of stone, jutting into the sky between the lower parts of the building, although 'lower' felt like the wrong word to use for walls twice as high as anything else in the city other than the outer barricades. He could just make out the distant shapes of guards patrolling up on the castle walls, protected by stone blocks topped with spikes. The top of every wall on the castle was spiked, meaning no dragon could land there. It vaguely reminded Rutger of the sharpened logs that had made up the wall protecting Gothendorf. Except these walls couldn't be burned, and were protected by more than a couple of idiots with rusty spears. He couldn't imagine any attacker getting past those walls, even with magic.

Meanwhile, down on the ground, Ring Street was bustling. Most of the buildings on both sides were shops, taverns or brothels. (He had never seen a brothel before, but it didn't take much effort to recognise one when he did.) Rutger still had a few thaler left, so he decided to browse through a few shops and see if he could buy some leather. He had packed a small toolkit; enough to make some basic items if he had the leather to work with. It would be a good way to make a little money while they were here.

The first shop he went into, though, was selling fruit and other fresh foods. The place smelt glorious; he stopped in the doorway and sniffed gratefully. It was nice to look at as well: the walls were lined with shelves which held wooden boxes full of apples, oranges, pears, carrots, peas in their pods, and a dozen other kinds of produce, some of which he had never even seen before. Jars of spices sat on the counter, and there were even flowers for sale — bunches of them sitting in huge earthenware vases.

Rutger picked up a couple of carrots to snack on, and went to look at the flowers. Maybe he should buy a bunch for Swanhild, to try to smooth things over between them. He didn't think he should really be apologising to her; after all, he hadn't said anything wrong. She had only snapped at him because she was unhappy here, so some flowers might cheer her up.

With that in mind, he chose a bunch of sweet-smelling red flowers whose type he didn't recognise. 'How much?' he asked the man behind the counter.

'Seventeen thaler for the roses,' the man replied. 'One half-thaler for the carrots.'

Rutger choked. 'Seventeen! How could flowers be that expensive?'

'Those aren't any flowers,' the grocer said indignantly. 'They are genuine roses, all the way from Gallia. You won't find a better price for that kind of quality anywhere else.'

Rutger shook his head in disgust while he examined the roses. He didn't care if they were magical flowers with the power to cure dysentery – nothing should cost that much. 'I'll just take the carrots,' he said, handing over the money for them.

'Fine,' said the grocer, clearly still annoyed with him.

Rutger stuffed the carrots into his pocket, deciding he may as well question the grocer anyway. 'So, tell me,' he said, 'I'm new here. Drachenburg is so close, so why don't the Jüngen attack here?'

The grocer snorted. 'What? Are you stupid? How can you possibly not know about that?'

'Because I just got here,' Rutger said patiently. 'That's why I'm asking.'

'They don't attack because Lord Ethelred has a treaty with them, that's why,' said the grocer. 'Obviously.'

'I don't see it written in the sky,' Rutger snapped back. 'What kind of treaty?'

'An agreement to leave each other alone — what else did you expect?' said the grocer. 'Are you going to buy anything else while you're here wasting my time?' He was already looking past Rutger toward a couple of other customers who had just entered.

'Fat chance,' said Rutger. He threw another disgusted look at the overpriced flowers, and walked out of the shop.

He had better luck at the next place he tried. Deciding it would be better to interrogate someone who had a reason to like him, he asked around until he found a tanner's workshop. There, it was very easy to get into a conversation, and it helped that the owner, a young woman, seemed naturally friendly and keen to chat to a fellow in the trade.

'So you're a tanner as well!' she said cheerfully, once Rutger had told her.

'That's right. I had my own workshop back home,' he said, looking around hers with a pang of nostalgia. Like all tanner's shops, it smelled, but not too badly, as with his own, the actual tanning wouldn't be done here. In any case the faint whiff of urine and other unsavoury substances used to cure leather didn't bother him. Various pelts hung from the walls: wolf, fox, rabbit, otter and even a couple of mink. Rolled-up deer and cow hides sat on racks at one side of the shop, and on the other side there were leather goods — clothes, belts, boots, bags and a dozen other things.

'What brings you to Trutzberg, then?' the woman asked, bringing him out of his thoughts.

'Just visiting,' said Rutger. 'How long have you been here?'

'Oh, my whole life,' said the woman. 'My name's Adela. And you?'

'Karl,' he lied. 'I was thinking that while I'm here I could buy some leather and make a few things — I could do with the money.'

Adela looked thoughtful. 'Well, if you want to make some money, why don't you do some work for me?' she said. 'I could do with the help, and I have all the tools.'

'That would be perfect!' said Rutger. 'When could I start?'

'Oh, right now,' said Adela. 'Show me what you can do, and maybe I'll ask you to come back tomorrow. How does that sound?'

'It's just what I need,' said Rutger. 'Thank you.'

She showed him to the back room, where her main workroom took up the back of the building. A long, scarred old bench took up the middle of the floor, and a good selection of tools hung on a rack. Adela had obviously just been in the middle of something; cut cow hide had been laid out on the bench and partially stitched, and the spool of thick waxed thread sat ready nearby.

'I have an order for six saddlebags,' Adela explained. 'You can see the pattern here already — show me how you handle it.'

It was a job Rutger had done before, plenty of times, and her pattern wasn't too different from the one he had used. He picked up the tools and got to work.

Adela watched approvingly. 'Yes, that's just right,' she said after a while. 'Good, I think you can finish it without any trouble. I'll get back to watching over the shop.'

She went back through the curtained doorway to the shop counter, but stopped to pull the curtain aside and hook it on a nail so that they could see each other.

While Rutger worked, he took the opportunity to talk. 'So tell me about Lord Ethelred,' he said. 'How did he make this treaty with the Jüngen?'

'Oh, that clever Brittainien,' said Adela. 'He has us well protected — him and his weapon. I don't reckon the weapon is real, though.'

'Why not?' said Rutger. 'And what weapon?'

'It's said to be something that can stop magic,' said Adela, 'but nobody's ever seen it. I think it's just a rumour Ethelred put out to make the Jüngen fear him.'

'But *something* stops them attacking Trutzberg,' said Rutger. 'What's that if it isn't a weapon?'

'A treaty,' said Adela. 'See, Ethelred and that Jünger Lord Warin had a meeting. They made some kind of agreement that Drachenburg would leave us alone.'

'But the Jüngen are our *enemies!*' said Rutger. 'They want to wipe us all out. What could Ethelred have offered them to make them stop?'

'Don't be silly,' said Adela. 'The Jüngen don't want us dead. They just want to live in peace like the rest of us. That's why they agreed to it. One day we might even be able to start trading with Drachenburg; that would end it for good.'

Rutger's stomach churned. He couldn't make himself believe it. The Jüngen had always hated Gottlosen, and the Drachengott's command was to kill every single one of them in his name. Warin wouldn't ignore that for the sake of a treaty. There *had* to be a weapon. Some kind of threat which Ethelred had been able to use to keep the Jüngen at bay. He must just be keeping it a secret from his people.

'If there's no weapon, then how did Ethelred kill those Jüngen assassins who came after him?' he asked.

He had to wait while Adela dealt with a customer before she replied, and when she did it was a careless: 'Oh, his guards probably killed them.'

'But the Jüngen have *magic*,' said Rutger.

'Doesn't make them immortal,' said Adela. 'A good spear through the gut can kill a Jünger just as it would for anyone else.'

Rutger gave up after that; she obviously didn't know anything more than she had said. But he kept on working steadily for the rest of the afternoon, until night fell and Adela announced that she was closing up shop for the day.

'You've done some good work here,' she said, inspecting the completed saddlebags. 'Will you come back tomorrow?'

'If I can,' said Rutger.

'Wonderful. Here's your pay for today's work. I hope to see you again!'

Rutger gratefully took the bag of thaler, thanked her and left for the inn, thinking that even if he hadn't learned too much he had at least made some money. Maybe that would cheer Swanhild up.

The thought of Swanhild immediately dampened his mood again. She might still be annoyed with him or, worse, she might have kept that coldness that had come after it. The idea depressed him. She had always been so warm and generous toward him, so her sudden withdrawal had been shocking as well as unpleasant. He almost wished he had bough the roses, if only because it might have made her smile again.

He went back into the inn, which was now very crowded, and wove through the tables to get to their room. Along the way, however, someone caught him by the sleeve. 'Karl!'

Rutger turned to see Swanhild, sitting at a table with some food in front of her. His stomach lurched at the sight of her. 'There you are,' he said blankly.

But Swanhild's smile was back, and it was real again. 'I've been waiting here for ages,' she said. 'Sit down, quickly, before the food gets cold and the beer goes warm!'

Rutger sat, still wary. 'I'm sorry,' he said. 'But—'

Swanhild pushed a mug of beer toward him. 'No,' she said. 'Don't apologise. I shouldn't have snapped at you like that.'

The knot in Rutger's stomach loosened. 'I'm sorry if I said something to upset you,' he said.

'You didn't,' said Swanhild. 'I told you: being here makes me nervous, and that made me irritable. I shouldn't have taken it out on you, and I've been feeling bad about it all afternoon.'

'You didn't have to,' said Rutger, although he was secretly touched that she cared that much about his feelings. 'I wasn't really upset.'

'Even so, it was no way to treat you after you gave up so much for me,' said Swanhild. 'But now: eat, drink, and tell me what happened!'

But Rutger didn't move. 'I would give up even more for you,' he said softly. 'I mean it.' The words were out before he could stop them, and he had to stop himself from saying even more.

Swanhild paused. 'Don't say that,' she said. 'I understand that you trust me, and that you … want to help me, but you shouldn't be prepared to throw everything away for the sake of one person.'

'That's not what I meant,' said Rutger, immediately embarrassed. 'I mean— That is, I wouldn't … unless you wanted me to. What I said before, in that office—'

'Stop,' said Swanhild. 'Slow down.'

But Rutger couldn't stop, not now. 'I meant what I said,' he told her. 'In that office, when I said I loved you so much I'd do anything for you. I wasn't just saying that to fool the official; I was telling the truth. I love you, Swanhild. With all my heart.'

There. It was said, and it couldn't be taken back. He felt half sick, but he had let go of those words that had been stuck inside him all this time, driving him mad. All that he could do now was wait. Wait, and stare into her rich, dark eyes, as if his entire life hinged on what she said next. And maybe it did.

Swanhild stared back at him for a long moment, and then looked down at the table with a troubled expression. 'I hoped … I hoped you would never say that,' she mumbled. 'But I knew … I was waiting for it.'

'Why didn't you want me to say it?' Rutger asked, with a stab at his heart. 'Is it because you don't like me?'

'No, I do … like you,' Swanhild said, quickly looking up. 'You're a brave man, and you're sweet. I've liked you since the moment we met. But I saw you were falling in love with me, and I dreaded it, but I didn't know what to do …'

'But if you like me, then what's wrong with it?' asked Rutger. 'Why can't we be together? Is it because of the war? Are you too afraid that we'll lose each other? Because I swear I'll never let that happen.'

'No,' Swanhild said sharply. 'You can't make that kind of promise. You know you can't. And you shouldn't want to be with me. There are too many things, too many secrets, things you don't know about me ...'

'Then tell them to me,' said Rutger. He reached over the table and took her hands in his. 'Tell me everything. You don't have to keep secrets from me.'

Swanhild hesitated. 'I'm ...'

'Yes?' said Rutger.

She looked away for a long moment, and finally said; 'I'm not someone who can ever be normal. I'm too different, too strange, too— Our worlds are too different, and we could never stay together. I would only break your heart, and I can't bear to do that.'

'No, you won't,' said Rutger. 'I don't believe that.'

'Well you should,' said Swanhild.

He smiled gently at her. 'You don't trust yourself, do you? You've lost too much to want to risk having that happen to you again.'

'No,' said Swanhild. 'The truth is that I never had anything to lose. Not until now.'

'I understand, but life isn't worth living unless you have something to lose,' said Rutger. 'Is it?'

She managed to smile back at him. 'No, perhaps not.'

'Then you shouldn't keep those things from yourself,' said Rutger. 'You deserve more, Swanhild. You deserve everything. And if I could, I'd give it all to you. All you have to do is trust me.'

Swanhild let go of his hands. 'Then I'll trust you,' she said. 'I'll tell you the truth. Something no one else knows. But we should go back to our room, for privacy.'

Rutger stood up, heart pounding. He felt almost giddy. 'Let's bring the food.'

Swanhild picked up the plate she had bought, and he carried the beers. In the relative quiet of their room, they put it all down on the little cupboard and sat together on Swanhild's bed.

'What is it?' Rutger asked her. 'What did you want to tell me?'

Swanhild leaned against him, staring straight ahead at the opposite wall. 'In all my life I've never told anyone this before,' she said. 'I suppose I was afraid that people would think I was strange or unnatural. But when you and I first met ... It wasn't chance. I was there that day because I was looking for you.'

'But how did you know about me?' asked Rutger, bewildered.

'Because I had seen you before,' said Swanhild. 'In my dreams. I have a power, you see — a power I have never seen or heard of in another person. I can see the future. Or parts of it. Sometimes I dream of things that will happen.'

'And you dreamed about me?' said Rutger.

'Yes,' said Swanhild. 'I saw you holding a weapon with the power to destroy the Drachengott, and I was there beside you. I knew that if I wanted to see him defeated I had to find you, and help you to find that weapon. So I went in search of you, and I found you. But I didn't know if I would be able to trust you at first. In the end,' she turned to smile at him, 'I saw that I could.'

'What else did you see?' asked Rutger. 'Did you see if I would defeat Warin? Did you see me fight the Drachengott?'

'No,' said Swanhild. 'But Ethelred's weapon must be yours. That much I did see. And I must help you. There.' She looked at the floor. 'I told you the truth.'

'And did you see us together?' said Rutger.

'Oh ... well ...' Swanhild smiled again, shyly. 'Perhaps I did, and perhaps I didn't. But some things you should decide for yourself.'

'Then I've made my decision,' said Rutger. 'Have you made yours?'

She sighed, long and deep and sad, and reached out to put her arms around his waist. 'Maybe you're right,' she said. 'I spent so long chasing a dream that I had ten years ago, and ignored anything else I wanted.'

'But you won't chase that dream alone now,' said Rutger. 'I swear.'

She smiled. 'No ... Now that's enough. Stop talking.'

When he started to speak again, she silenced him with her lips.

Chapter 15

They never got around to eating their dinner that night, or even sleeping very much. When morning came and they could finally bring themselves to get up, they breakfasted together on the leftovers. The bread had gone dry, the vegetables had shrivelled and the meat had congealed, but to Rutger it was the best meal he had ever eaten. He couldn't stop looking at Swanhild, and the mere sight of her filled him with a joy unlike anything he had ever known in his life before. It was as though his whole body was enveloped by a delicious warmth. Everything seemed lighter now; jokes were funnier, smiles were wider, laughter was a pure delight. To him, the world felt *right* now. Everything was complete, everything as it should be, and nothing could ever truly go wrong. And if it did, it was nothing he and Swanhild couldn't fix so long as they were together. Even the war with the Jüngen and the closeness to Drachenburg and its ruler couldn't upset him.

For her part, Swanhild looked just as happy as he felt. She kept looking at him and smiling, and reaching out to touch him at the slightest excuse, as if she couldn't stand to lose contact with him.

'So tell me what you learned yesterday,' she said eventually, almost lightly, as if it didn't matter much now.

'I found a job,' said Rutger. 'Earned some money. The woman said I could go back today and earn some more.'

'Woman!' Swanhild laughed. 'A woman, is it? And what exactly were you doing for her, then?'

Rutger laughed, too. 'She owns a tannery: I stitched some saddle-bags for her.'

'Ah, very good,' said Swanhild. 'I knew your skills would come in useful. Did you find out anything about Ethelred? Or this weapon?'

'Not much,' said Rutger. 'Most people seem to think it's simply a peace treaty keeping the Jüngen away. The woman I worked for even thinks Warin is interested in being a good neighbour to a city of Gottlosen! She didn't think Ethelred's weapon even existed. But I don't believe that.'

'Nor do I,' said Swanhild. 'We both know the Jüngen would never agree to keep away unless they were under threat. The people I spoke to yesterday said similar things.'

'Did you find out anything more than I did?' asked Rutger.

'Some things,' said Swanhild. 'They say that Ethelred came here from Brittainia as a young man, at the height of the fighting with the Jüngen. Trutzberg was close to being wiped out, but Ethelred had some way of defeating them. His famous weapon, obviously. He saved the city and was made its new ruler, and since then the Jüngen have kept away. That was a long time ago, so no doubt many believe the stories of what he did are exaggerated. Maybe he even tries to encourage people to think so, to discourage anyone from trying to steal his weapon. But now, I have a plan.'

'Yes?' said Rutger.

'If this tanner offered you more work, then you should go back there,' said Swanhild. 'Earn more money and see if you can take a permanent job there. Meanwhile I'll see if I can find work at the castle. From the inside, I can learn more about Ethelred. I can use magic discreetly, to make myself seem like such a fine worker that I'll be promoted. In time I may be able to get into Ethelred's private chambers and see this weapon for myself. Or I could seduce him,' she added with a wicked grin.

Rutger laughed. 'I think I'd prefer it if you were cleaning his floor!'

She kissed him on the cheek. 'Don't worry, Rutchen; I'll keep my distance from him. But what do you think of my plan?'

'It could take a while,' said Rutger.

'Are we in a hurry?' asked Swanhild.

'Not if there's no threat of Warin breaking the treaty,' said Rutger. 'But we don't know what he's thinking. I think we should go to Drachenburg. Meet up with that contact Haedwig told us about.'

Swanhild nodded. 'You're right. But let me do that. I've passed myself off as a Jünger before, I can do it again. There may even be Ketzer spies in Warin's castle; I can speak with them.'

Rutger frowned. 'I don't want you to go there alone.'

'But it would be the safest way,' said Swanhild. 'I would only be done for two days, and once I came back here—'

'But what if something happened to you?'

She smiled. 'I can take care of myself. I wouldn't take any unnecessary risks.'

'And while you're doing that, what will I be doing?' said Rutger. 'Staying here and making saddlebags? No — if you go, I'm going as well. I don't care if it's dangerous,' he added. 'I can't fight back against the Jüngen if I never take any risks. Anyway, I killed a dragon, didn't I? I can take care of myself, too.'

Swanhild held up her hands in mock-surrender. 'Fine, fine, I hear you! Let's both go, then. But first we'll use today to learn more about Ethelred's weapon. If I don't have the time to work my way in there legitimately, I'll have to find some other way.'

'So you're going to break into his castle?' said Rutger. 'I don't think—'

'No, I'm going to talk to some of his servants,' said Swanhild. 'Find someone close to him and bribe the information out of them if I have to. You're right that we need to take risks, but there's no need to take unnecessary ones.'

'All right, then I may as well go back to work and earn some more thaler,' said Rutger. 'You'll need something to pay them.'

Swanhild nodded with a quick smile. 'Don't worry,' she said. 'I'll be in no more danger than you — less, most likely, since I won't be using sharp tools.' She stood up as he did. 'Let's go to work.'

Rutger kissed her on the cheek. 'And with some luck I'll have a surprise for you tonight,' he teased.

'And I'll have some for you, I hope,' said Swanhild, with a sparkle in her eyes.

*

Rutger went back to Adela's leather shop and worked through that day in a happy little dream, scarcely even paying attention to what he was doing. When he jabbed himself with the awl — a common but painful accident that normally made him swear — it suddenly seemed amusing rather than aggravating.

'You're in a very happy mood today,' Adela said when they broke for lunch.

'Yes, I am,' Rutger answered through a cheery grin.

'I've been listening to you humming all morning,' said Adela. 'Badly. What's so good in your life, then?'

Rutger flinched, but then chuckled; he hadn't even realised he had been humming. 'I'm in love,' he said truthfully.

Adela paused with a piece of cheese halfway to her mouth. 'That's sweet,' she said. 'What's her name?'

'Swanhild.'

'That's a pretty name,' said Adela. 'Well, good for you. Just please stop humming, all right?'

'No promises,' said Rutger.

'You'll promise if you remember that I can dock your pay,' Adela said darkly.

Despite the threat, Rutger hummed and whistled to himself for the whole afternoon, all the while happily looking forward to seeing Swanhild again that evening. And when Adela paid him, she hadn't docked him after all.

'Come back again sometime,' she said. 'I might need help again.'

'I'll remember,' Rutger promised. He strolled out of the shop, singing a happy little ditty from his childhood, not caring if anyone stared. Nothing else mattered, not now.

Back at the inn, Swanhild had just arrived and had ordered them some food. Rutger ran to her, and they embraced passionately, both ignoring the hoots from the drinkers nearby.

'Come on,' Swanhild said when they finally let each other go. 'I can see a free table in the corner.'

They sat down facing each other over the food, but before they started eating Rutger opened the bag he had carried with him from the leather shop. 'I got something for you,' he said. 'Here.'

Swanhild took the gift with surprise. 'Are these ... ?'

'Roses!' said Rutger. 'I made them myself.'

She fingered a petal. 'You made me a bunch of leather roses?'

'I know they don't smell as nice, but they'll last forever and the real ones are way too expensive,' said Rutger. 'Do you like them? Adela even gave me the leather scraps for free.'

Swanhild laughed and hugged him. 'I love them! And I don't care that they don't smell like real roses; they mean more. Thank you.'

'It was a fun challenge,' said Rutger, kissing her. 'And all I could think about the whole time was how pleased you would be. Adela wanted me to make more of them for her to sell in her shop!'

'You should!' said Swanhild. 'But this time let's eat our food while it's still good.'

They ate, constantly glancing up to smile at each other. The food tasted even better than their breakfast had, although that might have been because it was fresh this time.

Once they had eaten, Swanhild gave him her news. 'It wasn't easy, but I managed to get into the castle kitchens,' she said. 'There were so many people working in there that all I had to do was pick up a basket of herbs and they mostly ignored me. When someone asked who I was, I said I was the new girl they must have heard about. It worked, too; people will do almost anything to avoid looking like they don't know what's going on.'

'And did you find anything out?' asked Rutger.

'Yes, I did,' said Swanhild. 'Ethelred's son came down looking for someone, and I got talking to him. Not so difficult; I flirted with him and he was happy to talk about anything I wanted. He told me all about his father, and the weapon. It's not exactly a secret, anyway.'

Rutger leaned forward eagerly. 'What did he tell you? What is it?'

'They call it the *Bealucræft Regnþéof*,' said Swanhild. 'It's Brit-tainisch for "Magic Taker". Apparently it's been in Ethelred's family for generations, and his son expects to have it one day. The son, Alfred, said it was nothing special to look at, but it can suck the magic out of any Jünger who goes near it. The process usually kills them, or leaves them powerless if they survive.'

Rutger shuddered. 'So why don't they use it to kill Warin?'

'Because Ethelred prefers to keep him alive and at his mercy,' said Swanhild. 'That way he can demand tribute in return for holding back. That's the other important thing I found out: there is no peace treaty — only a stalemate. Warin must want to attack, but he's afraid to, perhaps partly because he thinks his death might wound the Drachengott. And Ethelred is happy in his city, believing that the Jüngen are no threat to him anymore.'

'It sounds as though they aren't,' said Rutger. He took a mouthful of beer, and rubbed a thumb over the bridge of his nose. 'It's more complicated here than I thought ... If we steal the Magic Taker, the whole of Trutzberg could be destroyed.'

'If we can take it at all,' said Swanhild. 'Magic users must have tried again and again, and all of them failed.'

'Then how do we do it?' said Rutger. 'And should we?'

'If we want to destroy the Drachengott, we must,' said Swanhild. 'But first we need to go to Drachenburg and find out what Warin's intentions are.'

'Then let's do it tomorrow,' said Rutger. 'I'm ready if you are.'

'Indeed I am,' said Swanhild.

Chapter 16

The Jüngen city wasn't far from Trutzberg at all — less than a day's ride, in fact — and Rutger had been able to see its silhouette in the distance from outside Trutzberg's gates. He and Swanhild took their deer back from the stable and set out again, along the river which went along almost the entire length of Drucht Valley.

But this time things were different. Where the ride to Trutzberg had been peaceful and the landscape green and undisturbed, along the way to Drachenburg they saw more and more signs of the destruction that must have taken place there. The farms that had once been there were now abandoned, many of them reduced to blackened ruins. There were very few other travellers around, and those they saw avoided them. Some wore the red gemstones of Jüngen, and Rutger glared at them.

There were dragons around as well. The further away from Trutzberg they went, the more dragons they saw, flying overhead in a sky which seemed completely empty of birds. They made the abandoned ground seem that much bleaker.

That afternoon they reached a spot where the river forked. On the far side the ruins of a city could be seen, its walls crumbling now and its castle half-fallen in. Dragons perched on the remains like crows on a carcass.

'It must have been a massacre,' Rutger murmured. 'All of those people. And everything else here ... They've destroyed everything.'

'Yes, and Ethelred did nothing to stop it,' said Swanhild. 'That's well-known. That city there was called Ritterstadt. It was destroyed ten years ago, by an army from Drachenburg. Barely a handful of people escaped. The rest were slaughtered.'

'And Ethelred did nothing to help them?' said Rutger.

'They sent to him, asking him to protect them, even before the attack began,' said Swanhild. 'But he refused. Out of cowardice or selfishness, who can say? It's just as well for him that nobody survived; if Ritterstadt was still here, its people would be his worst enemies by now.'

'How could he be so cold?' Rutger wondered aloud.

'He must have had his reasons,' said Swanhild. 'But we would have to ask him to know for certain. Now ...' She reached into her pocket, and tossed him something. It was a small cloth bundle, and when he opened it a chunk of red stone on a plain silver chain fell out into his hand.

Swanhild was already putting on a second one. 'They'll identify us as very low-level Jüngen,' she said.

Rutger put on his with distaste. 'Will they accept us without any questions?'

'It should be easier than getting into Trutzberg,' said Swanhild. 'All we have to do is demonstrate our magic and speak a couple of passwords which I know. Listen carefully: when someone asks "What is the purpose of the Drachengott?", the correct answer is "To give purpose to the faithful". Then they'll say "What is the direction of the flame?", and you answer "To spread outward and cleanse all of Wendland". Repeat it.'

Rutger did, several times, until he had it by heart. 'So they'll just ask us that?'

'Yes,' said Swanhild. 'They're traditional questions Jüngen use to identify each other.'

'And if anyone asks who we are?' said Rutger.

'Why, a couple out for a pleasant day's ride, of course,' said Swanhild.

'I don't know about pleasant,' said Rutger, eyeing the derelict farmlands on their side of the river.

'So long as the company is pleasant,' said Swanhild, winking at him.

That cheered him up a bit, but he couldn't shake off his nervousness as they approached Drachenburg. The city looked dark, even up close, and although it, too, was surrounded by walls, they weren't topped by spikes. What they were topped with instead was dragons. Hundreds of them, perching overhead and peering down malevolently at anyone who came up the road to the gates. They were all about the same size as a human, and came in a range of colours. Some were brown, some green, some white or sky blue. There were a few rusty red, some grey or mottled. But all were horned, all spiked, all radiating savagery and danger.

Rutger's skin prickled under their gaze, and his sapphire throbbed as magic rushed through his system. He channelled some to his hands, ready to use it at the slightest excuse. Surely, any moment now they would recognise him as a Gottlosen and close in for the attack. And when that happened, he would go down fighting by Swanhild's side.

None of the dragons moved. There were more of them by the city gates, sitting on their haunches among a squad of Jüngen guards. None of the guards were armed — they wouldn't need weapons — but they were armoured, in heavy steel and leather.

Rutger could feel his deer trembling, and he dismounted before going any closer. The animal might panic just by being forced to go near the dragons.

Swanhild dismounted, too, and both of them held their deer firmly in case they decided to bolt or buck. The dragons stared at the pair of them as they came closer, and the nearest, a slate-blue dragon with pale golden horns, hissed softly.

Swanhild gave the beast a stony look, and walked on past. Encouraged, Rutger followed. The stone felt very heavy around his neck.

The human guards looked at them without much interest. 'What is the purpose of the Drachengott?' one asked in a bored voice.

'To give purpose to the faithful,' said Swanhild.

'And what's the direction of the flame?' said the man, looking at Rutger.

'Er, to spread outward and cleanse all of Wendland,' Rutger said hastily.

'Go on, then,' said the man, waving them past.

Rutger walked on past, greatly relieved, and Drachenburg opened up before him.

In some ways it wasn't so different from Trutzberg. But in others it was very, very different. There were paved streets underfoot and houses on either side, but these streets were lined with metal posts taller than a man, each one with a blue magical flame perpetually burning at its top. Above, dragons perched on rooftops. Some were down on the street, freely mingling with the people, all of whom wore red stones. Every now and then Rutger would feel a faint tingle in his chest as someone used magic. Up until now Swanhild was the only other person he had seen use magic since the night of Horst's death, but now he knew — he could *feel* — that he was surrounded by magic users. As he moved further into the city and began to see shops and other places of work, he saw the evidence as well. There were flame-poles here, too, although now the flames were green, and everywhere he saw people using magic, and not even for anything that looked very important.

He saw a stall where a woman was selling roasted chickens, casually cooking each one with a quick blast of magic before she handed them to her customers. There was a man repairing a pothole in the road by filling it with loose stone and then melting it together. There another man selling blocks of ice which he made himself on the spot. And there, two women linking hands and using their combined energy to make flowers grow for the benefit of people who brought them empty pots of soil.

'Most humble worshippers are given only the most basic powers,' Swanhild explained in an undertone. 'Enough to light a fire and make a living. Their stones are too small to contain enough energy for anything more.'

'Can they have their stones replaced, then?' asked Rutger. 'If they are given a higher station?'

'No,' said Swanhild. 'Once inside you, your stone can't be removed without killing you. Warin's must have been large to begin with. Or perhaps your stone can be made to grow inside you; that's something only a very high-level Jünger would know.'

Rutger imagined his sapphire expanding in his chest, crushing his organs, and grimaced. 'Do you know where this place is that Haedwig told us about?'

'Yes, it's this way.' Swanhild turned down another street, where the flames were yellow. 'If you ever get lost, you can use them to navigate,' she said, pointing to the flames. 'They're a different colour on every street.'

'I like that,' said Rutger. 'It's clever. And it looks pretty as well. I never knew magic could be used like this.'

'Well, why not?' said Swanhild.

'*I* can't think of a reason,' said Rutger.

The Twisted Lip inn turned out to be on the west side of the city. Rutger and Swanhild tied their deer to the hitching post outside and went in. It was a cheery place, very well lit by magical flames sitting in little alcoves in the walls. Rather than a fireplace it had another, much larger magical fire burning on a kind of pedestal in the middle of the floor, its flames a brilliant cherry red. People sat on the benches which ringed it, warming their hands and sharing food and drinks. At the bar, a weedy bald-headed man with an enormous nose was busy serving.

'That's him,' Rutger said immediately.

'How could you tell?' Swanhild laughed. 'Come on, let's go and talk to him.'

They went over, and Rutger opened his money bag. 'Two beers, please.'

'Right away.' The little man filled a couple of mugs and pushed them over. 'Five thaler.'

'Excuse me, but are you Egbert?' Rutger asked as he paid.

'That's me,' said the man. 'Heard of me?'

'From a friend,' said Swanhild. 'She said we should come and see you.'

'Oh, yes?' said Egbert. 'And what was her name?'

'Haedwig,' said Swanhild.

Egbert barely reacted to the name. 'You know my cousin?' he said smoothly.

'That's her,' said Swanhild. 'She was looking well the last time we saw her.'

'Happy to hear it, I am,' said Egbert. 'Well, if you have a message from her, just you wait here and I'll be back in a moment.' He took Rutger's money and walked off as though nothing had happened.

'He's good,' said Rutger. 'You would never think he was up to anything at all.'

'A man like him has to be good at hiding his thoughts,' said Swanhild, 'or he doesn't last long.'

A moment later Egbert came back. 'Now, before you hire the room you should look at it,' he said in a slightly raised voice. 'Step this way, please.'

They left their drinks at the bar and followed him to the stairs in the corner of the inn, which led up to a second storey. There were a few rooms up there, all apparently empty. Egbert ushered them through one of the open doors, and immediately closed it behind them. 'What is the purpose of the Drachengott?' he asked, turning to Swanhild.

'To enslave and to blind the faithful,' she answered.

'And what is the direction of the flame?'

'Outward, to destroy everything in its path,' said Swanhild.

'I thought so,' Egbert said grimly. He had an accent Rutger had never heard before, and clearly wasn't a native speaker of Wendish.

'It's good to see you,' said Swanhild. 'And as I said, Haedwig is well. She and her friends are well on their way to Ketzergard by now. We met them on the road, and they gave us your name.'

'That's good to hear,' said Egbert. 'Now, what is it you want? Make it quick: I have to get back downstairs.'

'What's the latest news on Lord Warin?' said Swanhild. 'What does he plan to do about Trutzberg?'

'That I don't know, but I do know this,' said Egbert. 'Warin might be here, but his blessed brother isn't. Reinhard is going east, toward Eidelstadt. He has an army with him. They plan to destroy Eidelstadt, then move on to Rintz and make that into a stronghold. Soon another army will make for Jarlsberg. By the end of it, there won't be anything left around Trutzberg but wasteland. That won't destroy Trutzberg or make Ethelred give up his weapon, but it will give him something to think about, won't it?'

'How in the world do you know all *that*?' said Rutger.

Egbert grinned at him. 'Army officers like a drink like everyone else. Anyway, is that it? Anything else?'

'Do the Ketzer plan to do anything about this?' asked Swanhild. 'Jarlsberg is very close to their stronghold.'

'Not that I know,' said Egbert. 'I think they still mean to keep their distance. But they wouldn't tell me their plans, not while I'm here.'

Swanhild chewed on her thumb. 'Can you send a message to them for me?'

'For the right price, I'll send them anything you like,' said Egbert.

'Fine,' said Swanhild. 'The message is this: tell Tanja that Ishild is in Jarlsberg and that now is the time to strike.'

Egbert looked shocked. 'Ishild? *The* Ishild? In Jarlsberg?'

'Yes,' said Swanhild. She took a handful of thaler from her money bag and offered them to him. 'This should be more than enough to pass that on. Be sure to make it as fast as you can.'

'Yes, yes, definitely,' said Egbert, stuffing the money in his pocket. 'Was there anything else you wanted to know?'

'Is that all you have?' asked Swanhild.

'Er ...' Egbert rubbed his huge nose. 'I hear Warin's having some troubles with his son. Thinks he might be a Ketzer sympathiser. I think that's all the latest news. But we'd better get downstairs now. Are you going to take the room or not?'

*

'Why are you so famous to the Ketzer?' Rutger asked Swanhild later, once they had settled down in their room at the Twisted Lip. 'Everyone looks so impressed when you tell them that you're Ishild.'

'I was a founding member of the Ketzer,' said Swanhild. 'One of the very first to join them when they were formed nearly ten years ago. The fact that I know Tanja personally is enough to impress most people,' she added lightly.

'What's she like?' said Rutger. 'And why did she form the Ketzer in the first place?'

'She was a Jünger, like all her family,' said Swanhild. 'But both her parents and all of her siblings were killed in an assault on the Gottlosen that went wrong. Her cousin Franz made the mistake of trying to surrender, and was declared a heretic and imprisoned. He was tortured, and kept alive only to be used as a sacrifice to the Drachengott. But Tanja decided she couldn't let her only surviving family die, so she rescued him and the other captives, and they fled from Drucht Valley. They were the first Ketzer.'

'Then when did you join them, if you were never a Jünger?'

'Tanja and her friends were looking for a place to hide, somewhere the Jüngen would never find them,' said Swanhild. 'We met by chance, in the wilds on the other side of the mountains, not so far from where you and I met Haedwig. I had found a perfect stronghold, and I showed them the way to it. Out of gratitude they let me join them, and Tanja gave me the gift of magic. But, as you know, we finally fell out when I wanted to give magic to other Gottlosen, and I left.'

Rutger rubbed the scar on his chest. 'Can Tanja be trusted? Will she really come to help us?'

'I'm not sure,' said Swanhild. 'She hates the Jüngen as much as we do, but she has no real love for Gottlosen either. She thinks of herself as a different and better order of human being because of her magic.'

'But ordinary people can be given magic as well!' said Rutger.

'Yes, which is why she regretted giving it to me,' said Swanhild. 'But she may choose to intervene in Jarlsberg, even if it means finally making her first move against the Drachengott. Sooner or later the time comes when words must give way to action.'

'I doubt anyone will survive if they don't,' said Rutger. 'And what are you and I going to do?'

'We have to go back to Trutzberg tomorrow, and warn Ethelred about Warin's plans,' said Swanhild. 'If he refuses to intervene, then we will have no choice: we will be forced to take his weapon from him, and use it ourselves to save those cities.'

'But how?' Rutger asked hopelessly. 'How do we take it?'

Swanhild smiled a rather nasty little smile. 'Don't worry,' she said, 'I think I know how.'

Chapter 17

They kept to their room that night, not wanting to draw attention to themselves, and left the Twisted Lip at dawn. The city gates had only just been opened, but they were allowed out without any questions, and they rode off together back toward Trutzberg as fast as they could. There, having quickly buried the Jünger necklaces at the bottom of their bags, they produced their papers for the guards and were let in without any trouble.

'Far too easy,' Swanhild muttered afterward. 'I wouldn't be surprised to find out that there are Jünger spies everywhere in the city. Biding their time, perhaps.'

'But that means they could strike the instant we took the weapon,' said Rutger. 'There has to be a better choice than stealing it.'

'There is, but it's up to Ethelred to make it,' said Swanhild. 'We can hope he will be reasonable. Just remember to stay with the plan.'

Rutger nodded; they had gone over it several times already.

'No magic,' Swanhild reminded him. 'No matter what. Even using it near the weapon could be fatal.'

'I know, I know,' said Rutger. 'I'll restrain myself. You should, too.'

'I'll try my best,' Swanhild smiled. 'Now then ...'

They left the deer at a stable close to the gates, and made for the castle on foot. By now the day was well advanced, and the shops on Ring Street had opened. The street itself was bustling. Rutger and Swanhild passed Adela's leather shop along the way, and Adela, busy hanging up some bags in the window, gave Rutger a cheerful wave.

Rutger waved back, but the sight of her made the weight in his stomach feel even heavier. If things went wrong today, he could be condemning her and all her neighbours and friends to death. He gritted his teeth — he couldn't let that happen.

As for Swanhild, she seemed calm enough, although he suspected she was as nervous as him underneath. She followed the street to the back of the castle, where a small gate hung open and a cartload of vegetables was being ushered through. Swanhild went right to the edge of the archway, waving at Rutger to follow. They pressed themselves against the wall, watching the pair of guards posted on either side of the gates. As the cart went in, though, both men left their posts to check it.

'Now!' Swanhild ordered in a low voice, and with that she and Rutger darted through and into the courtyard on the other side. Rutger's first instinct was to keep running, but the moment they were well away from the wall Swanhild slowed to a casual walk and he imitated her.

Sure enough, there were no challenging shouts from the guards or anyone else.

'You see?' said Swanhild, a trifle smugly. 'Look as though you belong, and most of the time people will treat you as if you do.'

'All right, we made it in,' said Rutger. 'But that was the easy part.'

'You wouldn't be saying that if we had been caught and thrown out,' Swanhild sniffed.

'No, I suppose not. Do you think we'll find him in the kitchens again?'

'I doubt it,' said Swanhild, 'but we can start there.'

The kitchen door was easy to spot. It was open, and people were coming out to collect the food from the cart. A delicious smell of baking bread came with them. Rutger sniffed it appreciatively — they had missed breakfast. Swanhild didn't hesitate. She picked up an armload of carrots from the cart, and joined the others. Rutger hastily shouldered a sack of flour and followed.

'What are *you* doing here?' a woman in an apron asked suddenly, frowning at him.

Rutger shifted the load on his shoulder. 'Oh, er ... I'm here with my sister,' he said, nodding toward Swanhild. 'She works here.'

'Hurry up, Karl!' Swanhild called back at him. 'I said you could see the kitchen only if you did something to help!'

Rutger gave the woman a quick, apologetic smile, and hurried to catch up with Swanhild. The woman followed, frowning at Swanhild now.

'I don't know you,' she said. 'What's your name?'

'Helga,' Swanhild lied. 'I'm new here, but you would have seen me the other day.'

The woman looked her up and down. 'Wait,' she said. 'I know what's going on here. You can't fool me.' She took in Swanhild's beautiful face, and shook her head. 'Honestly, who does that man think he is? First the maids, and now the kitchen as well?'

'I'm sorry?' Swanhild said politely.

'Don't you try and flatter me with pretty manners,' the woman snapped. 'I know what you're really doing here. You're one of that brat

Alfred's harem. Oh, he thinks he's clever, that one does — planting his girls in the castle staff so he can have them on hand whenever he pleases. I saw you talking to him last time. Do you even know how to cook?'

Swanhild smiled thinly. 'I can cook … Is Alfred nearby?'

'He will be as soon as he knows you're here,' said the woman. 'But who said you could bring *this* specimen along?' She glared at Rutger.

Rutger glared back while he did some quick thinking. 'I came to have a talk with this Alfred,' he said. 'To make sure he's treating my sister properly.'

'He isn't; trust me,' said the woman, although her expression softened. 'All right, you can stay here and help out until he comes by. But I don't want you back again, understand? A few useless girls with pretty faces are one thing, and I can't do anything about them while Alfred's around, but this is still my kitchen.' She glanced down at the sword hanging from Rutger's hip. 'And you won't be talking to anyone while you're carrying that — put it down over there.'

'Understood,' said Rutger, sweat beading on his forehead.

'Then take that flour over there to the storeroom, and go collect the rest of it. Hurry up!'

Relieved, Rutger unbuckled his sword and hung it from a hook, then carried the flour into the large, stone-lined storeroom which led off the kitchen. Swanhild followed, still carrying her carrots. 'Well done,' she said in an undertone. 'You're very good at this.'

'I just play along with you,' Rutger murmured back.

'Well now, all we need to do is keep ourselves busy until my Lord Alfred comes by,' said Swanhild. 'And I think he will.'

She and Rutger got to work, helping the kitchen hands finish unloading the cart. After that Swanhild was ordered to chop some vegetables while Rutger had the tedious job of stirring a pot of soup.

Still, at least it gave him the opportunity to keep his eyes open and watch for any sign of Alfred. If Alfred had seen Swanhild here recently and she had flirted with him, he might well come back in the hopes of finding her here again. For the time being, he and Swanhild were stuck.

The day wore on, and Rutger grew more and more impatient. The Jüngen might be attacking Eidelstadt at that very moment, while he was busy sorting a bag of hazelnuts.

He waited until Swanhild was nearby, and took the opportunity to whisper: 'How long are we going to keep wasting our time with this?'

'As long as we have to!' Swanhild snapped back. 'We can't sneak off and look for him without being seen.'

'But he's not—' Rutger began.

At that moment Swanhild stiffened as someone came up behind her and put a hand on her waist.

'Helga! There you are.'

Rutger tensed and backed away. The intruder was a young man with shiny, dark brown hair. He wore a fine red velvet coat and a ridiculous hat with a feather in it, and he was already touching Swanhild's back and shoulders as though she belonged to him. Rutger's fists clenched.

Swanhild smiled brightly. 'My Lord Alfred, how wonderful to see you again!'

The nobleman smiled back, but it came off as something closer to a self-satisfied smirk. 'I came back here looking for you yesterday, but you weren't here. I was so disappointed.' He had the same accent as Egbert, but his voice was rich and smooth.

'I wasn't feeling well yesterday,' said Swanhild. She ran a hand down Alfred's arm. 'But I feel much better now.'

Watching her flirt with the man made Rutger want to scream. It took all his self-control to stand by and do nothing, but Alfred must have noticed the filthy looks he was getting because he let go of Swanhild and confronted Rutger. 'And who are *you*?'

Swanhild took him by the arm. 'Alfred, this is my brother, Karl. He wanted to meet you.'

Alfred looked disdainfully at Rutger. 'Yes, and what do you want?'

Rutger coughed. 'My sister told me about you,' he said. 'But I wanted to see you myself, to be sure that you are treating her properly.'

'He's a little overprotective,' Swanhild said apologetically. 'Pay no attention to him.'

'Rest assured, my little Wendish friend: your sister is being *very* well-treated here,' said Alfred. 'Now, be off with you.'

'I promised him he could have a day's work here in the kitchens,' said Swanhild. 'To fill in for me.' She put an arm around Alfred's shoulders. 'Let's just leave him here and go somewhere more private, so we can get to know each other better. Please, can we do that?' Her voice was soft and beguiling, and would have melted Rutger in an instant if she had used it on him.

It worked on Alfred as well. He smirked again. 'Yes, of course. Let's go, my dear. Karl, you stay here and get back to work on those hazelnuts. Don't worry — you'll have your sister back in one piece.'

Swanhild let him steer her out through the door where Rutger's sword hung, but she threw a quick glance back at him and mouthed *come on*.

Rutger didn't waste any time in obeying her. The moment she and Alfred were out of the room he darted over to the door, ignoring the cook's complaint, snatched up his sword and buckled it back on as he followed them.

A short corridor led to a dining room, where Alfred had just started trying to embrace Swanhild. But the moment Rutger arrived she let go of him and backed off. 'That's enough,' she said.

Alfred gaped, and then growled. 'What's he doing here? I told you to stay back there!'

'We need to speak with your father,' said Swanhild. 'Immediately. We have information for him about the Jüngen.'

Alfred half-laughed. 'You *what*?'

'We need to meet with your father,' Rutger repeated. 'It's urgent.'

'You most certainly are *not*—' Alfred started to say.

Swanhild cut him off. 'Lives are at stake,' she said. 'You understand? Unless we speak to your father, people will die. The whole of Trutzberg could be destroyed while you're here wasting your time with cheap women.'

Alfred stared blankly at her. Rutger waited for him to banish the pair of them, or summon the guards, or say something pompous and stupid. His sapphire tingled, and he put a hand on the hilt of his sword, ready to do what Swanhild had suggested would be necessary, and take him hostage.

But when Alfred spoke next, he said the last thing Rutger had expected. 'What information do you have?' he asked cautiously. The petulance had left his face, and he looked suspicious but worried.

Even Swanhild looked slightly surprised. 'The Jüngen plan to take Eidelstadt, and then Rintz, and Jarlsberg,' she said. 'With those places captured or destroyed, Trutzberg will be surrounded. Your father's weapon can't stop the city from being starved out if they raze the farmlands, which they most likely will. We need to speak to him immediately, and tell him that.'

Slowly, Alfred reached up and took off his hat. He scratched his head with his free hand, frowning. 'Where did you hear that?'

'From an informant in Drachenburg,' Rutger said honestly.

'Then who are you? Jünger spies?'

'No,' said Swanhild. 'We work for the Ketzer. Tanja, their leader, wants to make an alliance with Trutzberg. Together, you can defeat the Jüngen. Alone, you will perish.'

Alfred tensed. 'You're Ketzer?'

'No — ordinary people,' said Swanhild. 'They wouldn't risk sending people with magic into Trutzberg. But we must speak to your father. Will you take us to him?'

Alfred straightened up, and adjusted his shirt. 'Yes ... He should hear this. Come with me, both of you.'

There were a couple of guards just outside the dining room. Alfred waved at them to follow him, and they did, stationing themselves on either side of Rutger and Swanhild. There was no escape now. But Rutger couldn't stop staring at Alfred.

'I can't believe it — he has a brain,' he whispered to Swanhild.

She winked at him. 'You can find brains in the most unexpected places sometimes.'

Chapter 18

They found the famous Lord Ethelred in the main room of the castle, where there were already plenty of people gathered. The ruler of Trutzberg sat on a fine carved chair up on a pedestal, with a pair of guards on either side and more near the main doors. Finely dressed people relaxed on benches by the walls or stood near the base of a large staircase, and Ethelred himself was in conversation with a man who looked like an official of some kind.

The ruler of Trutzberg looked just like an older version of his son, with the same shiny dark hair, wide forehead and pointed nose. He wore a dark blue velvet robe trimmed with yellow silk, but that wasn't what caught Rutger's attention about him the most. The moment he laid eyes on him, Rutger could feel the faint tingle of magic that hung around the lord. His sapphire throbbed in response, and he quickly started to search for any sign of the weapon. He couldn't see anything that looked like a weapon of any kind, but maybe it was hidden somewhere, in his sleeve or at the back of his belt ...

When Alfred came in, his father looked up and stopped his conversation. 'Hello, my son — what is it? Who are these people?'

Alfred stopped at the base of the pedestal, and bowed. 'Father, these two people need to speak with you immediately. They have important information for you, which you should hear in private.'

Ethelred stood up, eyeing Rutger and Swanhild. But then he said, 'Very well — leave us.' He waved at the nobles and officials, who left in ones and twos, many of them casting curious looks back at the visitors. Only the guards stayed.

'Now then,' Ethelred said as soon as they were alone, 'say your piece.'

Swanhild glanced at Rutger, and stepped forward toward the chair. 'My Lord Ethelred,' she said, bowing. 'My name is Ishild, and I came here on behalf of Tanja, leader of the Ketzer, with a message for you.'

Ethelred tensed immediately. 'What do the Ketzer want?'

'To warn you,' said Swanhild. 'The Jünger lord Reinhard is marching on Eidelstadt and Rintz. His brother Warin plans to attack Jarlsberg.'

Ethelred barely blinked. 'And Trutzberg? What do they plan for us?'

'To surround you and starve you out, most likely,' said Swanhild. 'You must act quickly. An alliance with the Ketzer could save your city. I'm here with an offer to act as your emissary to Tanja.'

'And are you a magic user?' asked Ethelred.

'No, neither of us are,' said Swanhild. 'Now that I have told you all that I know, perhaps we can come back later to hear your reply?'

Ethelred came down the steps from his seat. 'No, that won't be necessary. I have your reply ready immediately: I will not ally with magic users, least of all traitors like the Ketzer, and I will not break my treaty with Lord Warin.'

'But what about Eidelstadt?' Rutger interrupted. 'And Rintz and Jarlsberg?'

The lord gave him a disdainful look. 'What about them? They can fight for themselves. Trutzberg will remain untouched; I have Lord Warin's word for that. If Eidelstadt can't defend itself, then so be it. Our intervention would bring the Jüngen down on all our heads.'

'But they're coming down on your heads anyway!' said Rutger. 'Once they have surrounded you, they will destroy your farmlands, and you will be forced to surrender!'

'And do you have any proof of that?' asked Ethelred.

'You fool!' Swanhild spat. 'Do you honestly believe that Warin will honour any promises he has made to you? The only reason he hasn't destroyed Trutzberg already is because of the Magic Taker, and you won't be able to use it against him after you have starved to death. The Jüngen will never spare any Gottlosen city. Not Eidelstadt, and not Trutzberg. If you stand by and do nothing, you're condemning not just your neighbours, but yourself.'

'And you expect me to trust you?' said Ethelred. 'When you came into my city and then my castle without permission, and lied to my face?' He reached for the belt hidden under his robe. 'You are a magic user, and you can't hide it from me. I have my ways of knowing.' As he spoke he took something from his belt, but it wasn't a weapon at all. It looked like a short metal rod tipped with a red gemstone the size of a fist, held in a special grip like a dragon's claw. But Rutger could sense the magic around it. He kept back, still guarded and with Alfred nearby.

'Now, Rutger!' Swanhild shouted.

At the signal, Rutger moved. Before either of the guards could react, he grabbed Alfred by the back of his shirt and pulled him backward. With his free hand he drew his sword, and pressed the blade against the young man's neck. When the guards tried to intervene, he wrenched the sword upward, slicing Alfred's skin open and making him whimper. 'Don't make me do it!' Rutger snarled. 'Hand it over, Ethelred. Give us the Magic Taker, or he dies!'

'Don't!' Alfred gasped.

Concern flickered over Ethelred's face. 'Let him go, right now!'

'Drop the weapon,' Swanhild ordered. 'Drop it and let us take it, or my friend will take off your son's head.'

'Don't do it!' said Alfred. 'The city matters more than me: let me die if you have to!'

Rutger had a moment to be impressed by the man's courage — but only a moment. Ethelred's grip tightened on the Magic Taker. 'No,' he said, and pointed the weapon at Swanhild. Instantly, silvery light began to glow around her. It flowed from her chest and hands, straight toward the red gemstone, which began to glow in turn.

Swanhild groaned and fell to her knees, clutching at her chest as the magic leached out of her. 'Rutger ...'

'No!' Rutger shouted. He tightened his grip on Alfred. 'Stop!'

Swanhild started to convulse, moaning in pain. Ethelred stood rigid, both hands clutching the Magic Taker, whose stone glowed silver — brighter and brighter by the second. 'Let my son go, and surrender,' he said. 'Now.'

'No.' Swanhild's voice was tortured, her face twisted as she slumped to the floor. 'No. You must live. You must—'

'Now!' Ethelred roared. 'Do it now: she only has moments to live. If you want to save her, surrender.'

Rutger hesitated, and the moment seemed to last forever. But what happened next happened in a heartbeat. With a strangled bellow of panic and despair, he shoved Alfred away and charged straight at Ethelred. Taken by surprise, the lord turned, raising the Magic Taker to defend himself. Rutger brought the sword down on it with all his strength. Metal met metal with a deafening clang, and the impact went slamming up through Rutger's arm, knocking him back. He staggered sideways, gasping, only vaguely aware of the shattered sword still in his hand. But he heard the faint chink of the Magic Taker's broken parts hitting the floor, and looked up to see Ethelred's shocked expression.

But his frozen horror lasted for only a moment before pure rage replaced it. 'You!' he screamed. 'You—!'

Half mad, the lord rushed at Rutger, but all the years of obsessive training came back to Rutger in that instant, and he instinctively pulled back and thrust. The sword blade had broken in half, but the remains were sharp enough. A long fragment of metal stabbed into Ethelred's chest and then broke off at the hilt. Ethelred staggered back with a cry, and Rutger ran to Swanhild. She had dragged herself over to the Magic Taker's broken remains, and clutched the stone in its holder to her chest. Silver light still glowed around it, but, as Rutger watched, it seeped back into Swanhild as she took it back. He took her by the shoulder and hauled her to her feet. 'We have to get out of here!'

Swanhild clutched at him. 'Run!'

Rutger had no time to think. He threw Swanhild over his shoulders and ran, still holding onto the broken sword handle. Nearby, Alfred was holding onto his wounded father, and the guards were closing in. Rutger sent a wave of force at them, throwing them back, and ran away up the stairs.

'Get them!' Alfred shouted after him. 'Kill them!'

Rutger had never felt more alive than he did then, that day when he was so close to death. Holding onto Swanhild's warm body, he ran faster than he had ever thought was possible, guards on his heels and magic pulsing through his veins. He didn't even think about where he was going; for now, all that mattered was to get away.

The steps led to a corridor lined with doors. Rutger ignored those and kept going to the far end, where an archway led to another set of steps, this one spiralling upward into a tower. He took them, staggering slightly, and burst out into the open air. A walkway at the top of one of the castle walls spread out ahead of him, and guards were already turning to see him coming. The rest were catching up, weapons drawn.

'Be careful!' one yelled. 'They're magic users!'

A guard threw a spear. Rutger knocked it aside with a quick blast of wind. Still acting on instinct, he put Swanhild down and threw down a pair of blue fires, one on either side of them, making a barrier between himself and the guards, who immediately fell back.

'Don't make me hurt you!' Rutger warned.

Beside him, Swanhild leaned on the ramparts. Her face was deathly pale and her eyes were half-closed. She looked nearly dead, and her voice was soft and sleepy. 'Fly,' she mumbled. 'Fly away, fly out of here.'

Rutger looked down. They were very high up, and any moment now the guards would pull themselves together and start throwing more spears at them.

'Fly,' Swanhild said again, still clutching the broken Magic Taker.

The wind ruffled Rutger's hair. He looked blankly at the broken sword hilt in his hand, and then stuffed it into his pocket. *Fly*, he thought. But surely ...

The guards had managed to reorganise themselves, although they were still holding back. 'Don't be afraid,' one of them said. 'They're cornered now, and their magic won't last forever.'

But maybe, Rutger thought, *maybe it can last long enough ...*

He didn't give himself any longer to think about it. He summoned up all of his magic, channelling it through his arms and legs, and as soon as it was ready he lifted Swanhild into his arms and hurled himself off the wall. The pair of them hurtled toward the ground — but only for a moment. Panicking, Rutger unleashed all of his magic in a massive blast of wind. It wrapped around them both, lifting them up into the sky, and Rutger's will to survive was all he needed. The sapphire already starting to burn inside him, he kept pouring his magic into the wind, wrapping it around himself and Swanhild and propelling them forward. They soared over the city, clothes and hair flapping wildly, as if they had been caught in a great storm.

In Rutger's arms, Swanhild started to laugh wildly. She spread her own arms as if to catch the air, and her own magic joined with his, strengthening the wind as it pushed them onward.

'Don't!' Rutger managed to say. 'You're too weak!'

But Swanhild only laughed. 'We're flying!' Her voice was full of ecstasy. 'You can fly!'

But they wouldn't be flying for much longer. Even with Swanhild's help, Rutger could feel himself starting to reach the limits of his magic. The burning in his chest grew stronger and stronger, until it hurt, and a terrible weakness started to spread through his body. Below the city had already passed away, and now they were floating over green fields. Rutger started to try to push them downward, hoping to land safely, but his magic was running low with terrifying speed. Red lights started to flash in front of his eyes, and his hearing and vision began to fade. Pain throbbed in his head, and the sapphire had become a hot coal in his chest. He groaned aloud.

Swanhild had stopped laughing. 'Rutger, stop!' she shouted. 'Take us down, now! Stop this, before—'

Below, Rutger could dimly see the silvery surface of a pond. He couldn't tell how far it was now, but it was too late. His magic gave one last feeble pulse and then stopped. The wind vanished, and they both fell.

Chapter 19

The impact woke Rutger up. A great cold splash enveloped him, and then he was gasping, splashing, struggling to swim. He had lost hold of Swanhild, and he could barely feel or see a thing. His mind and body had been gripped by an exhaustion so profound that part of him wanted to just let go — to relax and let himself sink to the bottom, where he could rest forever. Anything other than fight on. But another, stronger part refused to give in. He swam blindly for the shore, until solid ground rose up beneath him and he dragged himself onto dry land. He collapsed face-first into the mud and lay there, unable to move, although his mind was screaming at him that he should be looking for Swanhild. What if she was still in the water, drowning while he lay here like this? Or worse, what if she hadn't landed in the pond at all, but had hit the ground beside it and been killed instantly?

With an agonising effort Rutger pulled himself up and looked back at the pond. He was just in time to see Swanhild climbing out, grey-faced and shivering. She came straight to him and slumped down in a sitting position. 'I hate the water,' she wheezed. 'Rutger, are you all right?'

Rutger let himself fall onto his back. 'I'm fine ... just tired.' Even talking took a painful effort.

'You should be,' said Swanhild. 'Here.' She held out a hand and summoned a small silver fire, grimacing as the magic left her.

She and Rutger huddled together beside the flames, both shivering badly from a combination of cold, exhaustion and shock. But they were alive. They had made it.

Neither of them spoke. Neither one had the energy, and, besides, there wasn't much to say just now. Rutger kissed Swanhild on the cheek and held onto her with silent gratitude.

'That was reckless,' she rasped, and then fell asleep, leaning on his shoulder.

Rutger said nothing. He smiled to himself and gently laid her down by the fire. Then, not caring where they were or whether anyone might spot them, he lay down beside her and slept as well.

*

By the time he woke up, night had fallen. He sat up, wincing at the ache in his back and limbs, and warmed his hands over the fire.

Beside him, Swanhild mumbled something in her sleep. He looked over at her, and was relieved to see that her colour had improved. She should be all right, or so he hoped. Something hard was pressing against his hip. He frowned and stuck a hand in his pocket. It was the sword hilt. The blade had been completely broken away in the fight, leaving nothing but a jagged edge. Rutger put the useless hilt down by the fire with a heavy heart. He had gone to Ethelred hoping to reason with him or, if that failed, to take the weapon without hurting anyone. But now not only had he probably killed Ethelred, but he had broken the Magic Taker in the process. His only hope now was that it could be fixed.

He looked at Swanhild again, and to his amazement the Magic Taker's broken end was still in her hand. Somehow, she had kept hold of it all this time. She must have held onto it like grim death. Rutger reached over and gently stroked her hair.

Swanhild's face twitched as he touched her, and she muttered again. This time he could make out the words. 'No, not my ...'

'Not your what?' Rutger asked, mostly just for the sake of it.

Swanhild's eyelids flickered open, and she looked blankly at him for a moment before she woke up properly and smiled. 'Rutger.'

Rutger helped her to sit up. 'How do you feel?'

'Very weak, but I think I'll recover,' she said, shuffling herself closer to the fire. 'And how are you?'

'The same,' said Rutger. 'You were so brave back there.'

'So were you,' said Swanhild. 'You truly are a brave man, Rutger — the bravest I have ever met.'

Rutger lost his smile. 'I'm a killer,' he said. 'I killed Ethelred — I'm sure of it. And his son ...'

'But you did it to save my life,' said Swanhild. 'And your own as well — he would have killed both of us.'

'That doesn't make me proud of what I did,' said Rutger.

'It shouldn't,' said Swanhild. 'But it might make you feel less guilty. And now we have the Magic Taker.' She relaxed her hand at last, and the stone in its holder gleamed.

'Do you think we can fix it?' asked Rutger, reaching down to cautiously touch it.

'I don't think it's actually broken,' said Swanhild. 'Here.' She gave it to him. 'Try it.'

Rutger took it, tensing instinctively as he touched the stone, but nothing happened. He could feel the magic inside it, and he held it up to the light to look more closely at it. It was surprisingly dull to look at, not even a proper gemstone like those the Jüngen wore. It looked more like a chunk of red-tinted crystal, still jagged and rough from the ground. The metal rod that had held it was mostly gone now, leaving only a short stump still attached to the claw holder. Rutger gripped it awkwardly and pointed the stone at the fire. Nothing happened. He tried to channel his magic into the stone, and the effect of that was immediate. The energy came down his arm and soaked into the stone, which started to glow – blue through red, which made it turn a deep purple. Rutger quickly stopped the flow, and the magic came back out of the stone and went back into him. 'Woah,' he muttered.

'What happened?' asked Swanhild.

'That never happened before: my magic came back. Normally it only goes one way.'

'Ah, so the Magic Taker can channel magic,' said Swanhild. 'That makes sense. But you should be able to let it go the other way. Let me try something.' She reached out and sent a small bolt of silver light at the Magic Taker. It hit the stone and was absorbed into it — but then it kept on going, through Rutger's hand and into his body. He felt the sapphire react to the new energy, and gasped. 'It worked!'

Swanhild looked satisfied. 'Then I was right,' she said. 'The Magic Taker can pull the magic out of a magic user, but since you are a magic user yourself that means you can not only take it from someone, but keep it for yourself. The stories were true; this is a formidable weapon. And not broken at all, luckily.'

Rutger examined the stone with amazement, and some nervousness. 'Can you imagine what would happen if the Jüngen got their hands on it?'

'Yes, and I don't like it,' said Swanhild. She huddled closer to the fire. 'You must guard it with your life. What you have in your hands now can kill any magic user, and not only that, but it will make you more powerful in the process. I wouldn't wish it to be in the hands of anyone other than you, my love.'

Rutger didn't let go of it. 'We need to find a way to disguise it,' he said. 'If only I could keep it inside my chest, with my sapphire.'

'This.' Swanhild picked up the sword hilt. 'It will be hidden in this. Set into the pommel.'

'You sound as though you already knew that,' said Rutger.

'I do,' she answered, holding the handle up to the firelight. 'This sword is what I saw in my dream. This handle, with a new blade, and the Magic Taker's stone was part of it. We need to find a swordsmith to fix the blade. The stone we can add ourselves, with magic.'

'Then I hope we can find a swordsmith in Eidelstadt,' said Rutger.

'Yes.' Swanhild gave the hilt back to him. She stared reflectively into the fire for a while, and then added: 'I can't believe you flew.'

'It wasn't easy,' said Rutger. He grinned to himself. 'I think I'd like to try it again one day, though.'

Chapter 20

Without their deer, and with no supplies, getting to Eidelstadt wouldn't be easy. But fortunately they still had one thing with them other than two broken weapons and the clothes on their backs: their money bags had survived the fall. Once they had rested and regained some of their strength, they set out walking, and eventually found the road to Eidelstadt. They followed that on foot for most of the next day, until they met up with a trading cart going in the same direction, and paid a few thaler for a lift.

During the tedious three-day journey that followed, Rutger couldn't stop thinking about what he had done in Trutzberg. Maybe it had been necessary to kill Ethelred, but when he remembered it he didn't just picture Swanhild dying on the floor. He also thought of Alfred. The man might be pompous and spoilt, but his courage was real, and he hadn't deserved to watch his father die like that. There was no chance of making an alliance with Trutzberg now. Surely Alfred would become its new ruler, and he would do everything in his power to take his revenge on Rutger, and on Swanhild as well. And if it came to it, would Rutger be forced to kill him as well?

But perhaps, he realised, that was something he should worry about later. For now there was the prospect of Eidelstadt and the quest to save it. He could only imagine how many people he might have to kill there.

It was enough to put him in a glum mood, and only Swanhild could cheer him up. She seemed sensitive to his feelings, and she was gentle and patient with him, something he was very grateful for. She must have guessed what he was thinking, but she said nothing about it. He was glad about that as well; she wouldn't want to be reminded that he had regrets for something he had done to save her life, even if they were justified.

'Do you know anything about Eidelstadt?' he asked her instead, on the last day, when the city was close.

'Uh, they make cheese there,' said Swanhild.

'Obviously,' said Rutger, watching the cow-filled fields pass by.

'Their ruler is a woman named Lady Mathilde,' Swanhild added. 'Her family has ruled Eidelstadt for a long time, I believe. I've never visited the city, though, so I don't know much more about it.'

Their travelling companion glanced back from his seat at the front of the cart. 'Lady Mathilde's a tough one,' he said. 'A trained fighter. She'll need to be, when the Jüngen come. But the city's well-defended. You'll see that for yourselves soon enough.'

'That's good,' said Rutger, thinking grimly of the ruins of Ritterstadt.

The trader had been telling the truth: Eidelstadt looked very well-protected indeed. The walls around it were thick and heavy, topped with thousands of sharp metal spikes and patrolled by dozens of guards. Plenty more were stationed outside the gates, and, although

Rutger and Swanhild didn't have to endure another questioning session since Swanhild had saved their papers from Trutzberg, they were still given plenty of suspicious looks and asked quite a few searching questions. But the slightly soggy papers, and possibly their grubby and dishevelled appearance, were enough to convince the guards to let them in.

Thankfully, even though they might have looked unimpressive, both of them had recovered from their ordeal and had the full use of their magic back. Rutger knew they would be needing it soon.

There were guards in the streets of Eidelstadt as well, well armed and patrolling for any signs of trouble, but the city itself looked pleasant enough. Rutger and Swanhild passed by a large cheese-processing centre, which featured a shop at its front which sold everything from blue cheese to cream. Unable to resist, Rutger bought two wedges of his favourite smoked cheese, and he and Swanhild munched on them while they went in search of a swordsmith.

'Sure, which one did you want?' said the first person they asked.

'One who can repair this,' said Rutger, showing him the broken sword hilt.

'That'd be all of them,' said the man. 'Just about. Look, just go to Spear Street. The weapon makers are all there. You'll find one you like soon enough.'

'Thanks,' said Rutger. 'Which was is Spear Street?'

He listened to the directions, and he and Swanhild followed them to the famous street, which was an impressive sight. Dozens of workshops lined it, housing everything from blacksmiths to swordsmiths, armourers and arrow-makers. And they were doing plenty of business as well. Everyone here seemed to carry a weapon of some kind, and sometimes more than one.

'I had no idea they were so warlike here,' said Rutger, 'but it's just as well.'

'Yes, they should do well when the Jüngen come,' Swanhild agreed. 'Now, let's see what we can find here.'

They started to work their way along the street, stopping to talk to every swordsmith they found. But the price for attaching a new blade to Rutger's sword turned out to be much higher than they had expected. The first two they asked gave prices that were well above anything they could afford. The third took one look at the hilt and said that it would be impractical to put a fresh blade on a cheap hilt and that it would be simpler and cheaper to buy a new sword.

Rutger took in the racks of new swords hanging on the walls. They all looked a lot more impressive than his cheap, inexpertly made weapon ever had. 'If I bought one of these, could you at least transfer the grip from my sword?' he asked. 'It has sentimental value.'

The swordsmith, a woman, examined it. 'Maybe. What's it made from?'

'Dragon horn,' said Swanhild.

The woman looked impressed. 'Genuine dragon horn? That's valuable stuff; you don't get many swords with that kind of decoration. Where did you get it?'

Rutger's chest tightened. 'I've had it since I was a boy,' he said.

The woman examined the hilt thoughtfully. 'Hmm ... If I cut the end off here, I could probably slide the horn straight off, and then ... Yes, it should be possible. If I put it on one of my incomplete swords, it won't cost you any extra.'

'How much?' asked Swanhild.

The woman named a price which would eat up almost every thaler they had. Swanhild and Rutger exchanged glances, but then Swanhild said, 'Yes, we can pay that. How long will it take?'

'Oh, I can finish it by tomorrow,' said the woman. 'The sword will already be made. Why don't you take a look at what I've got and choose one?'

There were several unfinished swords hanging up at the back of the workshop, and Rutger went to examine them. The blades hadn't been polished yet, but they were still fine and sharp, properly shaped and balanced. These were swords made by a professional, not a village blacksmith. Rutger checked each one, searching for one about the same length as his sword had been. He found one that looked close, and pointed it out. 'That one.'

'You want a one-handed blade, then?' asked the smith.

'Yes, that's right,' said Rutger. 'That's what my sword was like.'

'Then it's yours,' said the woman. She lifted it down. 'Come back in the morning, and I should have it ready.'

Rutger left the sword hilt with her, and he and Swanhild left the shop. 'Well, we're almost broke now, but at least I'll have a new sword,' he said.

'The weapon is more important than money, or anything else,' Swanhild said sternly.

'Yes, you're right,' said Rutger. 'But now we should find somewhere to stay that we can still afford, and decide what to do next.'

In the end they couldn't find an affordable inn, so instead they bedded down in an abandoned stable and ate a basic meal which Rutger put together. At least he was able to use magic to heat it up, which made the situation a bit more pleasant.

'It will do,' said Swanhild. 'We might have to find work again to-morrow, though, if we're going to stay long.'

'Yes, but first we should warn this Lady Mathilde,' said Rutger. 'And this time we should do it without mentioning the Ketzer. In fact, maybe we should simply tell people on the street and let the news spread.'

'It might be easier,' Swanhild said wearily. 'And perhaps Mathilde already knows: a large Jüngen army coming this was would be hard to miss. But I'm too tired to want to even think about it right now. Let's get some rest, and let what comes come.'

Rutger nodded; it was tempting to just let things be for now. He barely seemed to have stopped moving since leaving Gothendorf, and, after all he had been through, the idea of letting all this go and finding a place to settle down had become very tempting.

'Wouldn't it be nice?' he said aloud. 'If we could forget all this and do what we told my family we were going to do? Find ourselves a home, get married and ... get on with our lives instead of getting involved in other peoples' affairs?'

Swanhild twisted a piece of straw between her elegant fingers. 'Once I would never have agreed with you, but now ... I know exactly what you mean. Before I had nothing else to turn to, but now, with you, I could imagine forgetting everything and finding another place to live. But we both know we can't do that. Unless someone resists who has the power to defeat the Jüngen and the Drachengott, then sooner or later the whole of Wendland will be overrun. And then there will be nowhere left for us to go.'

'You really think they would do that?' said Rutger, knowing it was a rhetorical question.

Swanhild didn't waste time answering it. It wasn't necessary to.

'Well, then,' Rutger said after a while. 'We can settle down afterwards. Finish this, and *then* find a home for ourselves.'

'Once this is over,' said Swanhild. 'Then we'll be free.'

It was a comforting thought, and Rutger went to sleep with it still in his mind. But at the same time he couldn't help but wonder how far away that day would be, and wish with all his heart that he could at least know for certain. Either way, he already knew with grim certainty that there never would be a normal life for him again. It was too late for that. Whether he won or lost, he would never be Rutger the furrier ever again. He would be someone else — had already become someone else. But who that person was, he couldn't tell.

Chapter 21

The next morning, Rutger and Swanhild woke up to find the city in a state of chaos. They heard the shouting and activity outside before they had even finished picking the straw out of their hair, and both of them hurried outside to find people everywhere, running back and forth, all carrying weapons. There was a note of anger and excitement in their voices.

Rutger grabbed the nearest person — a girl clutching a bow and arrows. 'What's going on?' he asked, although he had a nasty feeling that he could already guess.

'Haven't you heard?' the girl answered. 'The Jüngen are coming! A whole army of them! They're coming this way, with their dragons. Everyone has to get ready! Where are your weapons?' She ran off without waiting for an answer.

'*Verdammte Sheisse!*' Rutger swore. 'We have to go and get the sword, right now! That woman had better have finished it.'

Swanhild's red-brown eyes had gone hard, and her mouth thin. 'Now is the time,' she muttered. 'Now, at last.'

Rutger nodded sharply and darted away, and she followed him, sprinting through the crowd, elbowing people out of their way when they had to. This was no time for good manners. Spear Street was even more chaotic than elsewhere, packed with people frantically trying to buy more weapons for themselves. Rutger nearly tripped over a boy carrying a spear twice as long as himself, and caught a cut in his arm from a carelessly held dagger. He shoved the holder away. 'Put that thing down, *dummkopf*!' He pushed on without waiting for an answer, and finally managed to get to the swordsmith's door.

Inside, the place had nearly been stripped. The swordsmith, looking harassed, was frantically selling off the last of her stock with the help of another woman who looked like her sister. It took Rutger several attempts to get her attention.

'What?' the woman looked distractedly at him. 'What is it? Oh, it's you. Yes, it's ready — you can grab it yourself.'

Rutger looked past her and spotted the sword hanging behind the counter. Sure enough, the dragon-horn grip had been fitted onto it and finished off with a plain metal pommel. He lifted it down, marvelling at how different it felt in his hand. Lighter, but more natural. He quickly tucked it into his belt, and handed over the money. 'Thank you,' he said. 'You did good work on it.'

'You're welcome,' the woman said absently.

Rutger managed to struggle out of the shop, to where Swanhild waited. She looked tense, but she relaxed as soon as she saw the sword. 'I was so afraid it wouldn't be finished in time. Quick, let's find a quiet place so we can finish it.'

That was easier said than done, but away from Spear Street they managed to find a narrow alleyway with some empty boxes dumped in it. Hiding behind the boxes, Rutger took the Magic Taker out of his pocket. Then he drew the sword.

'Let me do it,' said Swanhild. 'You need to save your strength.'

'I'm not sure I'd be able to do it anyway,' said Rutger.

Swanhild chuckled. 'You can *fly*, Rutger. But never mind: let me see if I can do this.'

Taking the Magic Taker, she laid it on the ground at their feet. Then, keeping a safe distance from it, she blasted it with silver fire. Rutger felt the intense heat, and quickly backed off. Scowling, Swanhild put more magic into her flames, which became denser and even hotter. The metal holding the gem began to glow, and then melted, falling away and leaving the stone itself untouched. Swanhild stopped her flames, and Rutger looked at the stone, and then at her, with concern. 'It didn't absorb your magic,' he said. 'Did it?'

'No,' said Swanhild. 'I thought it might, but ... I think it must work only when held by someone. Now ...' She sent a blast of cold air at the stone where it sat in a puddle of molten metal. The metal hardened, and she picked up the stone. It looked much smaller by itself. Rutger wordlessly held out the sword, with the blade lying across his palms and the pommel pointing toward Swanhild. She put her own hand on the pommel, and he felt the faint thrum of magic. Then, slowly at first but gradually speeding up, the pommel began to open. Cracks spread down its surface, and it peeled open like a flower blooming. The solid metal inside crumbled and fell away, leaving it hollow. Swanhild took her hand away, and thrust the stone into the hole she had made. It fitted perfectly, and she made a quick, satisfied noise and put both hands over the metal strips surrounding it. They bent inward, closing over the stone and almost completely hiding it from view.

Swanhild sagged on the spot as she took her hands away. 'There,' she panted. 'It's done.'

Rutger examined the sword with fascination. The pommel looked larger now, and it was a little misshapen, since the stone inside wasn't perfectly round. But the metal hid most of it, and the stone itself was only visible here and there, little chinks of red showing through polished steel. Swanhild had smoothed the whole thing, and it fitted into his palm very comfortably. The sword felt lighter now, and it would handle differently, but that didn't matter. He wouldn't need to use it the traditional way, perhaps ever.

'Do you like it?' asked Swanhild.

'Does it look the way it did in your dream?' said Rutger.

'Yes,' she said. 'Yes, it does. And it's yours, my Rutger.'

Rutger held the sword up, pointing it skyward. 'For my brother. Horst,' he said. 'For Ritterstadt. For Gothendorf. For us.'

'Yes,' said Swanhild. 'Yes—' But her voice broke suddenly, and she turned away from him.

Concerned, Rutger put the sword back through his belt and went to her. 'What's wrong?'

Swanhild's eyes were wet with tears. 'It's nothing,' she said. 'Don't worry about it.'

'Why are you upset?' he persisted. 'Was it something you saw? You didn't dream about this, did you?'

'No.' Swanhild smile weakly. 'No, it's fine. I'm just ... I'm afraid.'

'It's all right,' said Rutger. 'I won't let anything happen to you, or me either. We're going to win today, I'm sure of it.'

'Yes, I'm sure we will.' Swanhild wiped her tears away. 'Come on: it's time.'

*

Outside the alleyway, the excitement had not abated one bit. People had climbed onto rooftops and balconies, busy setting up caches of arrows and buckets of water. Others were wetting the thatch or shingles on their own roofs, hoping to fireproof them, while still more were carrying their valuables outside and burying them or hiding them in outdoor cellars. Rutger could feel the fear in the air.

Up on the city walls, other weapons could be seen. Giant bows, all surrounded by soldiers who must be preparing them. People were stringing up ropes and chains between the buildings, to hamper the dragons when they inevitably came, and the city guard were helping them.

Rutger automatically turned to Swanhild. 'What should we do?'

But Swanhild shook her head. 'From now on, the decisions are yours to make,' she said. 'We go where you choose.'

'Then ...' Rutger touched the sword hilt. 'Then we should go to the city gates. They will break in there first, and I want to be ready for them.'

'Then that's what we will do,' said Swanhild. And when Rutger walked away toward the gates, this time it was she who followed him.

*

There were plenty of others already at the gates of Eidelstadt. A squad of soldiers had drawn up in two rows just inside, all carrying spears, bows and other long-range weapons. They were only lightly armoured; Rutger supposed there wasn't much point in wearing steel when your enemies could melt or shatter it. Overhead, a net of chains had been put up to protect them from whatever might arrive come from the sky, and the gate was being reinforced with barrels and sandbags. Ordinary citizens had gathered as well, behind the soldiers, all armed and ready, and above the gate some men had been stationed with what looked like pots of boiling oil. The first Jüngen through the gates would regret it.

Rutger and Swanhild couldn't get past the people already there, so they joined the armed citizens at the back, and waited.

And waited.

The time dragged by. The soldiers finished building the barricade behind the gates, and the oil bubbled in its pots. People talked nervously, or simply stood in silence, gripping their weapons. Rutger left his sword hooked through his belt, half sick with anticipation.

'I wish it could be over,' he said eventually. 'Anything has to be better than this.'

'We'll see,' Swanhild murmured back.

When the attack came, however, it caught them by surprise. The dragons were the first to arrive. One moment there was silence, and the next a hundred dark shapes had dropped out of the sky and hit the chain net. People screamed or cried out, and a second later a hail of arrows shot up toward the dragons as they struggled to get through the net. Some died, and their bodies fell through onto the heads of the defenders, who scattered to avoid them as more, living dragons slipped through the holes in the net and attacked. Rutger leapt out of the way and drew his sword. With his left hand he shot magic at the nearest dragon, shattering the creature's wing. The dragon screamed and came on at him, only to be cut down by a couple of soldiers. Two more dragons slaughtered a man to Rutger's right and then turned on him, but they were too slow. Swanhild struck one with a blast of force, crushing it into the ground, and Rutger speared the other one with ice. In all the confusion nobody seemed to have noticed their use of magic, and even if they had there was no time to think about it. In a moment the defenders were overwhelmed, as dragon after dragon broke through the net and attacked them, scattering or killing everyone in sight. Other dragons ran to the barricade and began to demolish it, spitting fire at the gates and at the guards above, who sensibly dived out of the way rather than waste their oil on fireproof creatures.

A dragon spat flame at Rutger. He pushed it away with wind, then struck the beast down with a bolt of wind to the chest which broke its breastbone. As soon as the dragon had fallen he ran toward the gates, but he was too late. A deafening explosion ripped the air apart, and before the sound had even hit him he was falling backward, hurled away by a wall of force that destroyed the gates, and the barricade, and threw the dragons and everyone else to the ground. Rutger hit the paved street with a sickening crunch, and coloured lights span through his head. He got up, staggering sideways with his sword still in his hand. While his vision cleared, he looked frantically around for Swanhild, and spotted her struggling to get out from under a fragment of the gates. He stumbled over and pushed it off her.

Swanhild got up, grimacing. 'Are you all right?'

'I think so,' said Rutger. He felt a wetness on his forehead, and reached up to touch it. A long gash had appeared at his hairline, and his fingers came away bloody. 'It's nothing,' he said.

Swanhild had collected a few cuts and bruises as well, but she looked well enough. She turned toward the gates, and Rutger turned with her, while around them the others struggled to recover. They were just in time to see the Jüngen arrive.

Hundreds of people, none armed but all armoured, came charging over the remains of the gate and the barricade, red stones glittering on their chests and magic glowing around their hands and chests. The soldiers on top of the gate hastily tipped over their pots of boiling oil, but it had almost no effect. A few Jüngen screamed and fell, but most simply blew the oil away from themselves and ran on. Behind them, Rutger could see more Jüngen — hundreds more. Panic surged in his chest, and he nearly froze to the spot, but Swanhild's voice intruded.

'The weapon!' she shouted. 'Use the weapon, Rutger! Use it now!'

A strange calmness came over him then. Ignoring the shaking in his arms and back, he planted his feet well apart and pointed the Magic Taker forward. The first Jünger to reach him laughed at the sight, and hurled magical flames at him. They came for his chest, but in mid-air they turned, pulled toward the sword blade and then into it, sucked into the metal like water through a straw. Rutger felt it come into the pommel stone and then pour up his arm as pure magic, filling his sapphire. In front of him the Jünger stood stock-still, his expression dumbfounded as the magic came surging out of him, sucked away into the sword and then into Rutger. He made a move as if to back away, but couldn't seem to move, and a moment later he started to shake and then collapsed and died at Rutger's feet.

Rutger could feel the man's magic filling him, sharpening his senses and filling the air with sparks of light, just as his own had done when it had first come to him. He started to laugh wildly. 'It works! *It works!*'

'Yes,' said Swanhild, in a strange, hypnotic voice. 'It works. This is your destiny, Rutger von Gothendorf. Follow it.'

And Rutger did. He charged in among the Jüngen, absorbing their magic left and right, and then throwing it back at them. Fire and ice leapt from his hands, bolts of wind broke bones as if they were twigs. Even the dragons which came at him stood no chance. Before long, there was a ring of dead Jüngen and dragons around him, and the rest had begun to retreat in fear.

'Get them!' Rutger yelled to the defenders, who had fallen back, too, confused and afraid. 'For Eidelstadt!'

His call was enough. The people ran to his side, and they started to drive the Jüngen back. Recklessly, Rutger ran out of the city and into the mass of the army beyond. Swanhild was forgotten. Gothendorf was forgotten. All that mattered was the surge and rush of magic, pure energy which came into him in a torrent, expanding the sapphire in his chest, widening his senses, giving him unnatural strength. The Magic Taker burned in his hands, but he felt no pain. He was invincible.

He never knew how many Jüngen died under his onslaught. Later on, the memory of that battle was a blur. All he knew was that he charged on, the people of Eidelstadt at his back and sides, until at last he came back to a kind of sanity and stopped to see the figure standing in his way. And when he saw it, his invincibility faded and something else returned to him. The boy in the forest, cornered and afraid, listening to his brother's dying cries...

Rutger stopped, breathing hard, the sword pointing at the ground. '*You*,' he said softly.

One of the two Jüngen he had seen that night in the forest stood there, as though he had been waiting for him. He was older now, and more finely dressed, but he hadn't changed so much that Rutger didn't recognise him. He wore black and red, and the stone around his neck was now part of a magnificent amulet shaped like a pair of golden dragons.

'Reinhard,' Rutger spat. 'I know it's you.'

The man watched him cautiously. 'Who are you?'

Rutger lifted his sword again. 'My name is Rutger von Gothendorf,' he said. 'My brother was Horst. You murdered him in Schwartz Forest.' He could feel his mouth twisting as he spoke, contorting into a wolf's snarl. 'I've waited a long time for this.'

Reinhard laughed at him. 'You think you can cut me down with that?' he said. 'A sword?'

'You think you can cut me down with magic?' said Rutger, all his fear leaving him. 'Go ahead and try.'

Reinhard raised his hands and hurled green flames at him. But, just as with all the rest, the magic flowed into the sword and then on into Rutger. He stood still, bracing himself, relishing the look of fear and shock on the Jünger's face. At last, the time had come. At last, Horst would be avenged. And then—

But then something began to go wrong. The sword continued to pull the magic out of Reinhard, but instead of falling down and dying the Jünger stayed where he was, frightened and unable to move, but refusing to die. And his magic did not run out. It kept on coming, more and more of it, coming on and on into Rutger's body. His sapphire started to burn again, and the feeling of ecstasy and power came back, but now it wouldn't stop. It doubled, and then tripled, and his feeling of invulnerability gave way to fear, and then pain, as he realised, too late, that he couldn't contain this much power. It was starting to kill him, and he couldn't stop it from coming, and as he felt his very soul begin to disintegrate, a terrible insight came to him. This was not Reinhard. This was Warin. The ruler of Drachenburg had decided to lead the attack on Eidelstadt in place of his brother, and Warin's supplies of magic were not his own. Rutger was trying to take the powers of the Drachengott himself.

No, he thought. *Oh no!* But he couldn't say it now, or anything else. His mind was falling apart. In moments he would be dead. Nothing could break the bond now.

Through fading vision, he looked ahead and saw Warin. The man looked as afraid as he was, and perhaps he, too, was doomed now. Surely this would kill them both?

But just as Rutger's knees began to buckle, something big and dark came out of the sky, and struck the Jünger square in the chest. He fell, and the flow of magic stopped. And Rutger pulled himself up in time to see it, as a lithe black dragon with a broken horn pinned Warin down and bit him to death.

Gasping in disbelief, Rutger stared. The dragon didn't linger over Warin's body. It turned, jaws dripping with the Jünger's blood, and stared straight at Rutger. Its eyes were burning red, and the sight of them brought the memories of that awful night rushing back with even more force than before. Hatred gripped him by the throat. With the Drachengott's magic still surging through his body, he pointed the sword and sent a powerful wind straight at the dragon. If his hands hadn't been shaking so badly he would have hit the creature in the chest and killed it instantly. As it was, his attack caught in the dragon's wing and hurled it backward. The dragon went tumbling head over tail, hissing, and Rutger came after it, sword raised. 'You, dragon – came back to your master, did you?' he shouted, too overwrought for anything approaching reason. 'I'll have your head as well, and your other horn!'

The dragon recovered itself, and Rutger prepared to finish the creature off. But the dragon did not attack him. It turned to look at him, and a voice spoke from out of the air. *Rutger,* it said. *Stop. Do you not recognise me?*

Rutger started. 'Of course I do!' he said. 'You're the dragon who killed Horst!'

I did not kill him, said the dragon. Its voice was female. *Both of us were left to die from the spiders' venom. I survived. All this time I have waited to take my revenge on Warin for summoning me and then abandoning me.* She turned to look at the Jünger's body. Around them the battle raged on, but the rest of the Jüngen seemed to have lost courage. *Revenge is sweet, yes?* said the dragon.

Rutger summoned up his magic again. 'Yes, it is,' he agreed.

The dragon took to the air. *I promised to tell you this,* she said. *My name ... is Syn.*

'I don't give a damn what your name is,' Rutger swore. He hurled more magic at her, but she avoided it and flew away without another word, leaving him alone on the battlefield.

Chapter 22

It was only later, with the battle won, that Rutger had the chance to go in search of Swanhild. To begin with he had no choice but to help the defenders drive the last of the Jüngen away, which they did under his leadership. Afterward, the victorious people of Eidelstadt marched behind him back to the city, all cheering and shouting his name. 'Rutger! Rutger! Rutger the Jüngens' Bane! Rutger Dragonsbane!'

'How did you do it?' several people asked him excitedly. 'Where did you come from?'

'I came to save you,' Rutger told them. 'I have the power to take magic from Jüngen, and I knew they were going to attack here ...'

His madness had begun to fade now, and he couldn't look at the bodies he passed. Could he really have done all that? But he had. He knew he had. That madman who had gone rushing through the Jüngen, slaughtering them left and right — that had been him. And he couldn't use the thrill of magic as an excuse. It had been him.

He looked around for Swanhild, but couldn't see her anywhere, and nor did he see her back inside the city, where people crowded around him, all wanting to see him, to talk to him, to ask him his name. Exhausted and vulnerable, he couldn't stop them from pushing him all the way to the castle, where a muscular middle-aged woman in a plain blue dress was waiting for him. Her brown hair was in a braid, and her grey eyes were stern as she looked at him.

'Who are you?' she asked.

'His name is Rutger Dragonsbane,' one of the people in the crowd said eagerly. 'He came to save us from the Jüngen!'

'I was asking him,' the woman said sharply, immediately silencing the man. She looked at Rutger. 'Well?'

'My name is Rutger,' he answered. 'I heard that the Jüngen were coming here to attack, so I came to help defend your city.'

'And how did you do that?' asked the woman, whom he knew must be Lady Mathilde.

He held up the sword. 'This sword can pull the magic out of Jüngen.'

'But I've been told you have magic of your own,' said Mathilde. 'The news has spread like wildfire. Is it true?'

'Yes,' said Rutger. 'I have magic.'

'Then are you a Jünger?' asked Mathilde. 'Or a Ketzer?'

'Neither,' said Rutger. 'I'm a Gottlosen, like you. I was given magic by ... by someone else, and I vowed to use it to help other Gottlosen.'

There was an outbreak of excited shouting from the crowd. Lady Mathilde looked cautiously impressed. 'So you were never a Jünger?' she said.

'No, never,' said Rutger. 'The Ketzer don't want Gottlosen to use magic, but we can if it is given to us.'

'You mean you have the power to give magic to others?' said Mathilde.

'Yes,' said Rutger. 'If I think they are worthy,' he added, remembering what Swanhild had said to him what now seemed so long ago.

'Well, then.' Mathilde smiled. 'You may be a stranger, but you saved my city, and you are welcome to stay here in my castle for as long as you want.'

'Let him stay!' people shouted excitedly. 'Make him our champion!'

'Are you interested?' Mathilde asked.

'I would be honoured,' said Rutger.

'Then, please, come in,' said Mathilde. 'A room will be prepared for you, and you will be given a seat of honour at tonight's victory feast.'

'Thank you,' said Rutger. 'But there's someone I need to find first.'

He searched for Swanhild. The whole city searched, all keen to be the one to find this mysterious woman who had given Rutger his powers. They searched Eidelstadt, and they searched the battlefield outside its gates, and Rutger searched with them. But all anyone ever found was a long leather coat lined with mink and stained with blood.

Alone in his finely appointed new quarters in the castle, Rutger hugged the coat to his chest and cried. And not just because he had lost Swanhild, but because of the things he had done that day, the awful truths he had discovered.

He was a killer. He had looked other human beings in the eye and had killed them, and he had even enjoyed doing it. He didn't even know how many he had killed. Was that what he had wanted? Was that what he had set out to accomplish when he had left Gothendorf? But— it had been exactly what he had set out to do, he realised. He had left with the intention of killing a man. It just never occurred to him how many others might die in the process. And worse, he knew with absolute certainty that this would not be the end of it. Other attacks would come. More Jüngen would arrive at the gates of Eidelstadt, or at Trutzberg, or at Jarlsberg. Just as Swanhild had warned him, the Jüngen would not rest until all of those who refused to bow to the Drachengott were dead. And when they came, it would be up to him to stop them. He was the champion of the Gottlosen now, as he had hoped to be. To refuse to fight would be to abandon them all. He had no choice anymore.

All he could do other than dread the battles to come was to wish that Swanhild was there. She would have understood, and she could have soothed his fears. But she was gone, and he couldn't tell where or why.

Still, he refused to believe she was dead. Unless he saw her body, he would never believe it.

'Swanhild,' he mumbled through his tears. 'Where are you?'

*

Far away from Eidelstadt, a black dragon with a broken horn flew west. The others had gone back toward Drachenburg, or on to the Drachengott himself, but the black dragon flew alone, as she always had. It was good to feel the wind under her wings again, but she flew without joy, on toward Jarlsberg. She needed to know what was happening there, to see if the Ketzer had decided to intervene or if they had left the city to its fate.

While she flew, she wrestled with herself. All should be well now. She had done just as she had set out to do. The first of the four had been found, he had been trained, and the weapon was in his hands. And now he had become all he needed to be, and was ready for when the day came. Her task now was to move on, to find the second and give them her guidance and help. But, although her reason said that this was what she must do, her heart said something else, and for the first time in her short life, tears flowed over her scales and where whipped away in the wind.

Rutger, she thought. *I did love you. Please ... forgive me.*

*

And miles away, to the north, the Drachengott lay on his mountaintop and felt the slow agony inside his massive body, as he had felt it every day for thousands of years. He shifted on his perch, talons grinding against the stone, and thought, *Soon. Soon now it will be over.*

The air felt cool against his old, flaking scales. He closed his huge eyes against the pain, and endured, as he knew he must. And waited, with all the patience of immortality, for his time to come at last.

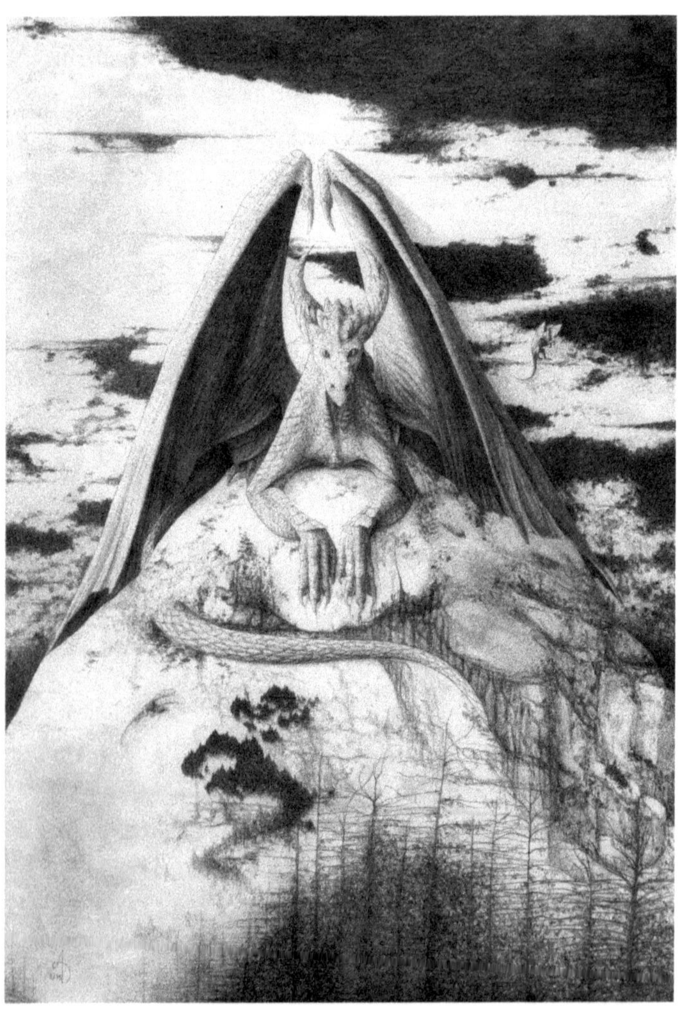

www.ingramcontent.com/pod-product-compliance
Lightning Source LLC
Chambersburg PA
CBHW040528170726
48295CB00012B/376